2020 Kind of Love

Melody Hadden

JAMBU Publishing — Hutto, Texas
ISBN: 979-8-9919756-0-5
Library of Congress Control Number: 2024924042
Title: *2020 Kind of Love*
Author: Melody Hadden
Digital distribution | 2024
Paperback | 2024

Dedication

I am dedicating this book to my husband, Josh Hadden. He has heard me talk about this book for 12 years. He was definitely my muse for John Hadley. I would also like to dedicate this book to my children, Caitlin, Logan, Lilly, Rose, Tyler and Lainey, and my sister, Sarah. She encouraged me to convert my handwritten book into a Word doc and she helped me do that as well.

PROLOGUE

My mother was sixteen years old when she gave birth to me. She recalls every detail of the day she went into labor with me. I have heard the story many times, but I always enjoy hearing it. My mother shares her enthusiasm when she tells stories. She shares her heart and soul. The day I was born was an exciting day for my young mother. She said I saved her life. I helped her to grow up and I gave her a purpose. She said before me, it was just her and her alcoholic mother.

My dad always said my mom could make a story about going to the gas station for a gallon of milk into a full movie. That is why this story was too hard for my mom to share with the world. I must tell the beginning of the story, until my mom regains her strength. She is extraordinarily strong because she has had to be strong.

There is not enough paper on the planet for my mom to describe her feelings for her husband and for the man that looked like her husband's murderer. That is where I will start this story….

CHAPTER 1
Chelsea

I was eighteen years old the day my stepfather died. We all loved him, but no one loved him as much as my mother did. She always said he was her soul mate.

"John's my true love, she'd say, smiling softly, not in that cliché way people throw the word around. "I don't mean perfect love. I mean real love. The kind that sticks."

They had married just six months after their first date. I'll admit, at first, I thought it was too soon. But John made my mother laugh like I hadn't seen in years. So, when he died, it was no surprise that she was shattered.

The day of the funeral was cold and wet. Too cold for early December in Texas. Mom stood by the casket, her lips trembling, but she didn't shed a tear. Not in front of people, at least.

"He wanted to see the Texas Lions make it to the championship," she murmured quietly to me, barely holding it together. John was obsessed with college football, second only to her. "It's cruel, him leaving before that."

"He'd be watching, though," I said, trying to comfort her. I wasn't sure if I believed it, but I knew she needed to hear something.

She shook her head, her voice cracking. "Not like this."

John had refused to attend weddings during football season. "Between August and January, you're out of luck," he'd say with a wink, waving off any other plans. When he wasn't with my mom, he was glued to the TV, yelling at referees like they could hear him through the screen.

Mom's life with John had been a second chance. After two failed relationships, including her marriage to my dad, she thought she'd never find love again. John was her lucky number three. They met on one of those cheesy dating sites, something neither of them expected to work.

"Can you believe this?" she asked me one morning, showing me her phone. "Some guy named John messaged me, and he's actually... normal. You know, like really nice."

I shrugged, not paying much attention. I was skeptical. After all, I didn't have the best track record with her previous relationships.

But then I heard her at night, laughing like a schoolgirl on the phone with him.

"Oh my gosh, John! That is hilarious," she'd say, barely able to catch her breath between giggles. I hadn't heard her laugh like that since... well, I couldn't even remember when.

One night, I woke up to find her sitting on the couch, still talking to him on the phone, her voice soft and full of warmth. "I know, right? My ex was the same. It's like they couldn't see beyond themselves."

She spotted me, put her finger to her lips, and winked. I didn't say anything, but I remember thinking: *Maybe this John guy is different.*

Soon after, they moved past messages and late-night phone calls. One evening, she turned to me, beaming. "John and I are meeting tomorrow."

"Tomorrow?" I raised my eyebrows. "That was fast."

She smiled, a little embarrassed. "We have been talking for weeks. It feels... right."

And it did. They clicked instantly. They were not like my mom's previous relationships, full of tension or awkward silences. John made her laugh and brought out this side of her I had not seen in a long time.

"It's like we're teenagers again," she said one afternoon, her cheeks flushed after hanging up the phone.

They got engaged within months. When I questioned it, she just smiled. "When you know, you know."

Even I could not argue with that logic—not after seeing how happy she was. And John? He was not like my previous stepfather. He had this charm about him, like a silver fox version of George Clooney but with a Fu Manchu. He treated my mom like she was the center of his universe.

When they exchanged their vows at the courthouse, John had whispered, "You will never have to doubt me, Christi. I am here for the long haul."

I was not sure what to say. I hadn't expected to feel so protective of her, but seeing her with John... it made me hopeful.

CHAPTER 2

I can still hear my mother's scream, sharp and raw, when the doctor told her John was dead. Her face contorted with confusion, her heart refusing to believe what her ears had just heard. She looked over at the other car accident victim's room, her eyes desperate for answers. Without saying a word, she walked in and sat beside the unconscious man lying in the hospital bed.

A nurse stepped in, hesitating for a moment. "Ma'am, can I help you with something?"

My mother didn't look up. She clasped the man's hand in hers, her voice barely a whisper. "I'm his wife... I'm here for him."

The nurse looked startled. "Excuse me, but... what's your name?"

"Christi Lynn Hadley," my mother said, her voice steady. "I'm John Hadley's wife."

The nurse's eyes widened in concern. "This man isn't John Hadley," she said carefully. "This is Jon Wright. His wife... she passed away about three months ago."

My mother blinked, as if the words didn't register. She tightened her grip on the man's hand. "There's a mistake. This is my husband. You've got the charts mixed up."

The nurse glanced at her with sympathy before excusing herself, murmuring, "I'll be right back, ma'am."

Minutes later, Dr. Pat Cook entered, his face solemn. He crouched slightly, speaking in that slow, soft tone people use when they're about to deliver terrible news. "Mrs. Hadley, I'm Dr. Cook. I'm very sorry to tell you this, but the man you're sitting next to is not your husband. His name is Jon Wright. I've known him for years. There's no way he could be John Hadley."

My mother's face flushed with disbelief. "No," she said firmly, standing up. "No. You don't understand. I just saw him. *This* is John."

Dr. Cook stepped closer, his voice even softer. "I know this is hard, but... will you please follow me?"

She shook her head, as though trying to shake off the reality creeping in, but she followed him, casting one last glance at Jon Wright before leaving the room.

I was pacing in the hallway, trying to keep myself together when I heard it—my mother's scream. It cut through me like a knife, raw and piercing, and I bolted toward the sound. By the time I reached her, she was standing next to my stepfather's body, her knees buckling as she leaned on the edge of the bed.

Her voice trembled, disbelieving. "Why are you doing this to me?" She looked down at John's lifeless body, her hands shaking. "How can this be? I just saw him... I just saw him in the other room!"

I stepped inside, my heart racing. Dr. Cook turned toward me; his eyes filled with the kind of quiet sorrow you see in people who have to deliver bad news all the time. He gave me a small, understanding nod, and I returned it before looking down at John's body. I started to cry.

My mind flashed back to our last conversation earlier that day. I had been in a rush, grabbing my keys on my way to work. John had stopped me just before I reached the door.

"I'm proud of you," he said, smiling that warm, familiar smile. "You're earning your own money now." Then, with a wink, he added, "You still owe me twenty bucks."

I had rolled my eyes, like I always did. "Tell you what—if I walk on your back, you forget about the twenty bucks."

His grin widened. "Deal."

He lay down on the living room floor, and I hopped up onto his back, pressing my weight into him. I tiptoed, jumped a little, and popped his back the way he liked. He groaned in relief.

Afterward, I stood there, looking down at him. "Love you, John."

He smiled that mischievous smile. "I love you more. And I said it first."

I chuckled, running out the door, never imagining it would be the last time I saw him alive.

Back in the hospital room, I sobbed as that memory played over in my mind.

Dr. Cook gently touched my mother's arm. "Mrs. Hadley, we need to check on you. Let's head over to triage for a moment, okay?"

She didn't respond at first, but after a long pause, she nodded. I followed them into the triage area, where a nurse in her early thirties took my mother's vitals. I could see the concern in her eyes as she read the results.

"167 over 101," the nurse whispered to Dr. Cook. They spoke quietly in the corner of the room, and Dr. Cook nodded in agreement before approaching my mother.

"Mrs. Hadley, we think it would be best if you stayed here for a while, just to make sure you're okay."

But my mother shook her head, her voice thick with desperation. "I need to see John... and Jon."

Dr. Cook hesitated, but then he let her go. We walked back into the room where John lay, cold and still. My mother stood there, her breath shaky, before walking out and heading straight to Jon Wright's room.

She took one look at him—just one glance—and then collapsed, fainting right there in the middle of the floor.

CHAPTER 3
Jon Wright

I love you too, Debbie. Wait—where are you going? Come back!" I reach out, but she slips away into the shadows. My eyes fly open, and I stare at the ceiling in the dark.
Just a dream.

She's been gone for over four months, and still, every night, I see her in my sleep. It's always the same—so close, and then gone. I roll over, checking the time. 3:30 a.m.

"Great," I mutter to myself. Another night without sleep. Another day where I drag myself to that god-awful job. I hate it—the routine. The grind. Every day is the same as the last.

I get up, walk to the kitchen, and stare at the bottle of vodka sitting on the counter. Debbie would hate this. *"You're drinking again at 1 a.m.?"* I can almost hear her voice scolding me.

"Sorry, Deb," I say out loud, uncapping the bottle. I take a swig, wincing as the sharp burn runs down my throat. It does nothing to numb the pain. Just another bad idea.

I slump against the counter, staring at the half-empty bottle. "What am I doing, Deb?" I whisper. "Why do I feel like I'm still waiting for something to happen? You're gone, and I'm stuck here."

My phone buzzes on the counter, but it's nothing. No messages. I glance at the time again—6 a.m.

Sighing, I head to the bathroom. In the mirror, I barely recognize myself. My eyes are dull, my hair's a mess, and the stubble on my chin is several days past a clean shave. *What happened to me?*

I turn on the shower, letting the hot water cascade over me, but it doesn't wash away the exhaustion or the grief. I go through the motions—dry off, dress in the same dull clothes, and stare at my reflection again.

"I'm a mess," I say to the stranger in the mirror. "Debbie wanted kids. I said no. Why did I say no?" I shake my head, frustration boiling up. "What was I so afraid of? Now, she's gone, and I'll never give her that. I'll never be a father because I waited."

My voice cracks. I grip the sink, squeezing until my knuckles turn white. "Would I really want to be raising kids without her?" The thought is too heavy, but it plays over in my mind every day, gnawing at me.

I try to shake it off as I head downstairs, but the house feels too quiet. Too big. I glance at the walls—Debbie's everywhere, in every picture. Our wedding day, her smile bright enough to light up a room. I can hear her laugh in my head.

I stop in front of the wedding picture, my heart aching. We wrote our own vows. I remember standing there, looking into her eyes as I said, "'Til death do us part."

I laugh bitterly. "We should've said, 'And not even death can part us.'"

My hand brushes the picture frame. "I wish there was a telephone in Heaven," I whispered, choking back tears. "I just want to hear your voice, Deb. I want to tell you I'm sorry… sorry for everything. And I promise—there won't be anyone else. No one will ever measure up to you. Ever."

The silence feels crushing, the emptiness of the house echoing around me.

I look at the clock, realizing it's time to leave for work. Another day of staring at numbers. Another day of pretending everything's fine when nothing feels fine.

I grab my keys, sighing as I head for the door. "Here we go again," I muttered. But deep down, all I want is to crawl back into bed, to find her again in my dreams.

CHAPTER 4
Chelsea

After my mother's collapse, the hospital moved her to a room and officially admitted her into the hospital. Dr. Cook examined my mother and that is when I learned my mother was expecting a baby. Wow, what a day that was. My mother was in her mid-thirties and had four children of her own, John's twin boys and now another baby on the way. I was afraid for my mother to wake up.

The doctor ordered a type of sedative for my mother, but eventually she was going to wake up and learn she was going to have a baby with her dead husband. As I sat beside my mother's hospital bed, just watching her sleep. I prayed for her; I prayed for our future and my unborn sibling. I was heartbroken knowing that this baby was going to grow up without the greatest dad that I have ever had.

The next morning my mother was already awake when I opened my eyes. I had fallen asleep with my head on her bed. My back was sore, and my head was pounding. My mother asked me what happened. I told her about her fainting spell, but I failed to mention her pregnancy.

My mother had a tubal ligation procedure about seven years earlier. She and John had talked about having another baby, but they never took the steps to having her tubal ligation reversed. So, this baby was already a miracle baby. A new nurse came in to check on my mother. My mother was eager to be discharged, but she was still just as eager to visit poor Mr. Wright.

The nurse indicated my mother could be discharged after a doctor came to examine her. The nurse also explained Mr. Wright was moved to ICU and that only his immediate family members would be allowed to see him. Dr. Warner came in and began to examine my mother. He made notations in her chart and told the nurse to discharge my mother.

The nurse left the room to retrieve the discharge documents. When she returned with the discharge instructions, she took the IV out of my mother's arm, and began telling my mother she should take it easy for a few days, and then follow up with her OB GYN. My mother appeared even more confused than she was yesterday. My mother asked the young nurse why she needed to investigate obtaining an appointment with her OB GYN.

The nurse must not have known that my mother was clueless about her pregnancy. The nurse told my mother she was sure everything was okay with "the baby," but it was still better to be safe than sorry.

As my mother began to say something, I interrupted her and said, "Mom, you're pregnant."

Tears were streaming down my mother's face. She was a lost little puppy with only me to help guide her.

I was eighteen years old yesterday morning, but I managed to age years in the last 24 hours.

CHAPTER 5
Jon Wright

I'm so glad to be finished with work. Time to swing by that drive-through liquor store and pick up a better brand of vodka than the last cheap bottle. If all goes well, I'll drink myself into oblivion and won't wake up until six tomorrow morning. How's that for a plan?

As I pull into the liquor store parking lot, I see her. The girl at the counter is young, thin, and blonde. She doesn't look a day over eighteen, but I know you only need to be that old to sell alcohol. She always tries to sell me a case of beer, but I can't stand the stuff.

"Hey there! Want to try a six-pack of our local brew?" she chirps, flashing a sales smile.

"Ugh, no thanks. Just give me the good vodka," I say, shaking my head.

"Sure thing! It's a great choice," she replies, ringing it up.

I quickly crack open the bottle and take a swig. Smooth. So much better than the cheap crap. I'll have to remember this brand for tomorrow.

Driving home, I don't have to sit in traffic tonight. I take a right onto Highway 79, heading toward Taylor, Texas—a small town that no one would brag about. The roads are rough, but they're finally doing maintenance. Thank God for small miracles.

But every bump reminds me of Debbie. I can still picture her laughing, tickling me as we drove to meet our realtor. We bought that nice three-bedroom house, and now it feels so empty.

"Why did you have to leave me?" I mumble to the empty car. "I miss you so much. I can't take this pain anymore."

I am thinking about getting a dog. Not that a dog would bring her back, but maybe a cute little puppy would help with the loneliness.

Suddenly, headlights appear out of nowhere! I jerk the wheel.

John Hadley

"What happened? Why am I staring at myself in my Ford Fusion? It's mangled and totaled."

"Who are you?" I asked, still dazed.

Jon Wright

"Who is she?" I hear my own voice ask, confused.

"That's Debbie!" I cried, my heart racing. "Wait, Debbie? Oh, my goodness, Debbie, what are you doing here? What is going on?"

Debbie nods her head and gestures for me to look at something. I follow her gaze and realize what she's showing me: my body—banged up and lifeless. Next to me, the guy in the other car looked dead. I'm not sure; maybe he's just sleeping. Am I really making jokes right now?

"What is wrong with me?" I whisper.

"Oh, Debbie, I love you! I've missed you so much!" I reach out to hug her, and she feels real. I can't believe it. She looks more beautiful than ever, even her smile brighter than I remember.

"Are you an angel?" I ask, hopeful.

"No," she says softly. "I'm here to walk with you. I'm here to welcome you home."

"Am I going to heaven?" I can barely breathe.

"Yes," she replies, her smile warm and reassuring.

But then the guy next to me—who I now recognize as John Hadley—suddenly cries out, "No! I have a wife and children! I need to see them again! I need to tell them how much I love them!"

I look at him, panic rising in my chest. Then I saw the vodka bottle in my car. John Hadley's eyes widen. "Were you drinking and driving?" he asks, a mixture of disbelief and hurt in his voice.

I feel a wave of shame wash over me. "Yes," I admit, barely able to meet his gaze.

He starts sobbing, a raw, heart-wrenching sound. "You have to fix this! You have to make it right!" He turns to Debbie. "Please, fix me!"

But Debbie can't help him. He rushes back to his own body, desperately trying to perform CPR on himself.

"What have I done? How can I enter the gates of heaven after killing a husband and father?"

Debbie's presence remains soothing, radiant; she doesn't feel the guilt or pain I'm drowning in. She's glowing, filled with happiness, while I'm lost in despair.

"I still have a pulse," I hear the emergency workers say.

"No! Don't touch me! Let me die! I'm ready to go with my wife!" I scream, but they can't hear me. They're focused on the other man.

John's eyes light up as he fights for his life. "My name is John Hadley," he gasps, as he attempts to tell me his name, but the realization is hitting him hard.

He knows. He knows he's not going home tonight. I'm happy and sad all at once. I cling to Debbie, refusing to let her go—not again.

CHAPTER 6
Chelsea

My mother and I sat at the kitchen table, poring over the details of John's funeral. The phone rang, and my mother's face brightened slightly as she answered it. "John's mother is driving in from San Antonio," she announced, a halfhearted smile on her lips.

When John's mother arrived, the atmosphere shifted. They embraced fiercely, both of them immediately breaking into tears. The sound of their sobs echoed in the air, heavy with grief.

"I can't believe this happened," John's mother said, her voice trembling. "My baby boy…"

I glanced at the kids playing next door with our neighbor, Jamie. I was relieved they weren't here to witness the raw pain radiating from their grandmother.

"Mom, tell her what you know," I urged, trying to help in whatever way I could.

Taking a deep breath, my mother began, "The driver of a Ford Fusion crossed the yellow divider and hit John head-on."

John's mother gasped. "What was the driver's name?"

"Jon Wright. He's in a coma at University Hospital," my mother replied, her voice breaking.

"What about John?" she asked, panic rising in her voice.

"He was... dead on the scene," my mother whispered, tears streaming down her cheeks. "It happened just three minutes from our home."

"Three minutes," John's mother echoed, her voice barely above a whisper. "Three minutes away from kissing him goodnight."

I could see my mother was trying to hold it together, but her eyes were lost in a whirlwind of emotions. "I saw him alive in one room," she said, her voice trembling. "Then, I had to see him dead in another room."

"Dead?" John's mother looked at my mom as if she were insane. "You mean you really saw him?"

My mother nodded, her face pale. "I know how it sounds, but it's true. I saw him..."

"And you're pregnant?" my grandmother interjected, her brows furrowing in confusion. "How?"

My mother shrugged, a look of resignation washing over her. "I don't know, Mom. It just happened."

My grandmother's expression was a mix of happiness and sorrow, a flicker of fear crossing her face. She sat down at the table, gathering her thoughts. "We need to focus on the arrangements," she said, her voice steady. "When will the viewing be?"

"Friday the 7th," I replied. "And the funeral service will be Saturday, December 8th."

CHAPTER 7

After John's funeral, I began noticing the strange, trivial things my mother was doing. Each morning, she would fill a glass half full of water and set it on John's nightstand. The next day, she'd wake up, roll her eyes, and exclaim, "Oh John, why can't you put your glass in the sink?"

This ritual continued, along with other odd behaviors. She never spoke of John as if he were truly gone. I could hear her crying softly at night, but in the daylight, she pretended he was still with us.

"Mom, you left the toilet seat up again," I would say, trying to lighten the mood.

"Oh, John," she would respond, as if scolding him for something he had done in life. It was as if she was trying to focus on the few things she found annoying about him, or maybe she was just lost in a world where he still existed.

I began to worry about her mental state. So, I decided to accompany her to her OB-GYN appointment. After all, I was one of Dr. Andrews' patients too. He had put me on birth control when my mother agreed it was time.

Dr. Andrews was a well-known figure in our community. He had delivered my three younger siblings and was in his early to mid-fifties, charming with a touch of ruggedness. He always wore cowboy boots with his scrubs, and he had this way of making even the most awkward situations feel comfortable.

As he examined my mother, I felt a wave of anxiety wash over me. "Where's John?" he asked, glancing up with concern.

My mother's eyes filled with tears, and I felt a pit in my stomach. "Oh no! I meant to tell him," I muttered, regretting not saying anything earlier. "Dr. Andrews, I need to explain. John… he passed away just two weeks ago."

Dr. Andrews quickly recovered from the shock, his professionalism kicking in. "Well, all the more reason to take care of this little one," he said gently, nodding toward my mother's belly.

We moved to a small room that felt even smaller with the sonogram machine inside. As Dr. Andrews prepared the equipment, I couldn't help but wonder what it would be like to see the baby. Then, to my surprise, he pulled out a wand that looked suspiciously like a male body part.

"What… is that?" I stammered, feeling my cheeks flush.

"It's for the sonogram," Dr. Andrews explained with a smirk. He placed a hygienic covering over the wand and prepared to insert it. "It's easier to view the baby in early gestation this way."

I blinked, trying to wrap my head around it. Just then, I saw Dr. Andrews' smile as he announced, "Two heartbeats!"

My heart raced. "What?" I gasped, my eyes widening.

He continued, "Baby A and Baby B."

"Oh, my word!" I exclaimed, my thoughts racing. My mother was going to have twins! It made sense;

John already had twin boys, so maybe it ran in the family. "He would've made a joke about right now," I thought, but the humor fell flat as the reality settled in.

I took a deep breath. John would've been ecstatic. He'd have found a way to lighten the mood, making my mother roll her eyes and laugh at the same time. But he wasn't here, and I was struggling to be strong for her.

"How far along am I?" my mother asked, her voice shaky yet hopeful.

"About seven weeks," Dr. Andrews replied, making notes on the screen. "I want to see you again in four weeks."

She nodded, though it seemed she barely understood what was happening. Dr. Andrews congratulated her before leaving the room, and she managed a polite smile, though I could see the uncertainty lingering behind it.

As the door closed, I opened my mouth, wanting to talk to Dr. Andrews about the strange behaviors my mom had been exhibiting. But in that moment, I was still too shocked by the news of twins to articulate anything.

CHAPTER 8

My mother must feel more overwhelmed than I do. I try to lighten the mood. I suggest we get lunch and do some Christmas shopping. My mother loves the food idea, but I am not sure about the shopping. We go to a Mexican food restaurant that is nearby. We have been there before, but the last time we went was with John.

My mother asked if she should order cheese enchiladas for John. I told her no.

She says, "You're right."

What in the hell is she thinking? We head to the mall; I am driving because I do not want her to get any bright ideas about joining her husband in Heaven. My mother bought the kids clothes, four Wii games and she bought a nice leather jacket. I asked her who the leather jacket was for. She tells me that it is for John.

Oh my, I wish that I had not asked her. I sure hope she is not planning to wrap this gift.

Later, that night I woke up to my mother's voice. She is praying aloud in her room. She says, "Father God I know that all things are possible for those who believe, please bring my husband back to me."

I am chilled at the thought of John's rotting corpse walking through the front door. I believe in the power of Faith, but this is one prayer that I am not holding my breath to be answered. I say a little prayer too.

"God please let my mother be okay."

CHAPTER 9
Jon Wright

John Hadley and I sat in the dim light of the car, the tension thick in the air. Debbie was with us, but she remained quiet, her expression thoughtful.

Finally, she broke the silence, her voice steady yet heavy. "There is a way for John Hadley to be with Christi again."

John leaned forward, hope sparking in his eyes. "Yes, anything. What do I have to do?"

Debbie glanced between us, her brow furrowing as she explained, "You can swap shells."

John and I exchanged puzzled looks, confusion clouding our faces. "What do you mean, 'swap shells?'" I asked, my heart racing.

"Your spirit is separate from your body, or your 'shell'," Debbie clarified. "John Hadley's shell… it's covered with a sheet now, but your shell still has a pulse."

I looked at John, my mind racing. "I want to be with you, Debbie. You want to be with Christi, right?"

He nodded, determination flickering in his eyes. "Absolutely."

"Then take my shell," I said, my voice firm. I reached for the vodka bottle on the floor and tossed it out of the car.

Debbie's gaze sharpened. "But you need to understand—John's blood alcohol level, which is technically your blood alcohol level now, will show nothing. His family will think you carelessly crossed that yellow line and killed him."

A wave of realization crashed over me. "Oh, my word, John!" I exclaimed, my voice trembling. "You are going to return in a body that your family will hate. They will blame you."

John's expression darkened as he contemplated the weight of my words. "I don't like that idea," he admitted, his voice barely a whisper. "But I want to be with Christi. I need her."

Debbie and I watched as he prepared himself to enter the shell. My body, lifeless in the back of the ambulance, felt so distant.

As he stepped in, I felt a strange warmth envelop me. I could hear the most beautiful music—a harmony so perfect it took my breath away.

Suddenly, I saw my family. My mom was there, arms wide open, hugging me tightly. A wave of joy washed over me. "I'm home," I whispered, my heart swelling with happiness.

CHAPTER 10

Chelsea

I t was Christmas morning, and the air was crisp and still. Inside, the house was warm, but there was a quiet heaviness lingering over us. John had been gone for three and a half weeks. His absence felt like a weight none of us could escape. His twin boys were with us for a few hours, their laughter and footsteps echoing in the halls. But soon, they would be going back to their mother's house, leaving an emptiness behind.

Mom looked radiant, despite everything. Her hand rested on her growing belly. "Dr. Andrews says the due date is June 25th," she reminded us, her voice soft but hopeful. "But with twins, it could be earlier."

I nodded, trying to focus on the future. "We'll be ready whenever they decide to come."

Mom smiled faintly, then glanced at the Christmas tree. The lights twinkled, but none of us could ignore the gap where John should have been.

"John's life insurance," I began, trying to fill the silence, "nearly a million dollars. That'll help, won't it? You can pay off the mortgage."

Mom nodded, her eyes misting over. "It's more than enough. And the other driver's insurance will settle soon too." She paused, swallowing hard. "It's a relief, knowing we're taken care of. John would have wanted that."

"Yeah," I agreed, glancing at the twins playing in the corner. "He'd be glad to know he's still taking care of you, even now."

We sat in silence for a moment, the only sound was the soft rustle of wrapping paper and the distant chime of Christmas music from the radio.

Then came a knock at the door.

On Christmas morning? We exchanged puzzled glances.

Mom stood up, wiping her hands on her apron, and walked toward the door. "Who could that be?" she murmured.

She pulled the door open, and her breath caught in her throat. I froze where I stood, my heart hammering in my chest.

"Oh my God," she whispered, her voice shaking. "John?"

There he was, standing on our front porch. Alive.

CHAPTER 11

John Hadley

I open my eyes, the harsh fluorescent lights above me making me squint. As I blink, trying to make sense of my surroundings, I realize I'm in a hospital room. The beeping machines and the sterile smell of antiseptic are unmistakable. A nurse stands nearby, but when I try to speak, no sound comes out.

"Hello, Mr. Wright," she says gently, noticing my movement. "My name is Kelly. I'm a nurse here at University Hospital. Do you know why you're here?"

Of course, I know why I'm here. Some loser drank a fifth of vodka, plowed into my car, and ended everything. He killed me and destroyed my perfect life. My perfect life.

God, I really did have a perfect life. Christi, my wife, and I were a perfect match. We never fought—not really. We made love almost every day, and when we weren't, we were laughing or planning our future. We loved each other in a way that was deep, real. We absolutely adored each other.

But now… what if I never get to make love to her again? What if I never get to feel her soft lips press against mine, or run my hands through her silky blonde hair? I try to push those thoughts away, but the memories flood in—memories of her, of us.

I remember our first date like it was yesterday. It was simple—she picked me up from work for lunch.

We went to this little deli down the road, nothing fancy, but it didn't matter. She was the most beautiful woman I'd ever seen. Christi wore this patterned red and white swirl, low-cut shirt with short blue jean shorts and black flats. Her straight blonde hair fell perfectly over her shoulders, her blue eyes sparkling. And those legs—God, those legs. Those shorts were practically made for her.

I couldn't take my eyes off her.

We laughed the whole time, mostly because she thought I was funny. And, well, I am. She laughed so much; it made me fall harder. After lunch, she dropped me back at work, and when she leaned in for a hug, I wanted to kiss her so badly. But I chickened out. I still regret that moment.

Later, I texted her. I told her how much I'd wanted to kiss her. And she replied, "I wanted you to kiss me too." That's just who she was—so cute and sexy, playing that sweet, innocent act when she wanted things to go her way, yet smart and sophisticated enough to always get what she wanted.

The next day, I asked her out again—this time for drinks and pool. When she came to pick me up, I asked her to come up to my apartment. The second I opened the door; I grabbed her by the back of the neck and kissed her like I'd been waiting my whole life for that moment.

She blushed, and I couldn't help but smirk. "That was worth the wait," I told her.

I still remember how she smiled at me.

We were on our way to the billiard hall when she told me how her biological father used to take her to bars when she was little. She became a pool shark by age nine. I don't know why, but the thought of her being that good at pool was... hot. Everything she did was. I wanted her so badly, but I knew I had to be a gentleman. She wasn't like any other woman I'd ever met, and she made it clear she wasn't just looking for a fling.

Nurse Kelly's voice yanks me out of my thoughts. She's talking again, but I can't focus on her words. She won't shut up. I would give anything to speak, to tell her to be quiet so I can think. What day is it? How long have I been like this? My eyes dart to the IV bag, where a handwritten date catches my attention: Dec 10, 2012.

I've been out for a week.

I need to know how Christi is. My hand clumsily reaches for the phone on the bedside table. My fingers fumble over the numbers, struggling to dial her cell. Finally, it rings.

She picks up. "Hello?"

My heart races. I'm here, baby. I'm here. I'm coming home to you. But no words left my mouth. She can't hear what I'm thinking, and even if I could speak, it wouldn't be my voice. It would be *his*. What good would that do?

I slam the phone down in frustration. Calling her won't help. I need to get better. I need to see her, face to face. And when I do, I have to convince her that it's me. That I'm her husband.

But how? How can I make her believe me? I think of our most intimate moments—those mornings after the kids left for school, when it was just the two of us. Moments no one else knows about. Will it be enough? Will the details of our life together convince her of the truth?

God, I hope so.

CHAPTER 12

Nurse Kelly walks into my room, a pitcher of water in her hands. The sight of it makes my mouth feel even drier, my throat like sandpaper. I'm so thirsty, I could drink the whole thing in one go if I had the strength. But as much as I want that water, something holds me back—my throat feels raw and tight, and I'm not sure I can even swallow.

She sets the pitcher down gently on the tray beside me, her voice calm and reassuring. "Mr. Wright," she begins, "you've been in a coma for a week. During that time, you were intubated—there was a tube down your throat to help you breathe since you couldn't on your own."

Her words hit me like a slow wave. A week? A whole week? My mind reels, but it's my throat that feels the worst. No wonder I can't speak. That god-awful tube had been in there for seven days, scraping against my vocal cords, leaving them damaged. Even though the tube is gone now, it feels like it's still lodged there, blocking my words.

But it's not just that. There's something else, something deeper. I feel… slow. Fuzzy. Like I can't quite remember how to speak, or even *who* I'm supposed to speak to. The panic sets in, a quiet hum in the back of my mind.

Before I can dwell too long on that feeling, the door swings open, and in strides a man with an iPhone in his hand, music blaring from Pandora. The upbeat rhythm fills the sterile room like it doesn't belong here, too bright and lively for a place like this.

"Hey there!" he says with a grin that stretches across his face. "I'm Reggie Jackson, your speech therapist."

I stare at him, still unable to speak, and he seems to pick up on that quickly. "Don't worry," he says, holding up his hands in mock surrender. "I know you can't talk yet, but we're going to work on that. In the meantime, I need you to blink once for 'no' and twice for 'yes.' That way we can communicate, alright?"

I blink twice.

"Perfect," he says, clearly pleased with himself. "Let's start with some easy ones." He pulls up a chair and sits next to me, looking me in the eye. "Do you know where you are?"

I blink twice.

Of course, I know where I am. I've been here before, years ago. It was the same hospital where Christi almost died. She had a tubal ligation before we met, but somehow, she still got pregnant. When she first told me, I was shocked. The idea of starting over with another baby in our advanced years—it scared me. But soon, I found myself getting excited. A kid with Christi's intelligence, personality, and athleticism, combined with my own charm? That would've been a blessing.

But then everything went wrong. She started having intense pain, a fever that wouldn't go down. I rushed her here, to this very hospital, and that's when they told us—an ectopic pregnancy.

I remember sitting in this same place, my heart breaking for her. But at the same time, I felt… relief. It's a feeling I'll always carry guilt for. We already have six kids. The thought of another one—it sounded impossible, like it would drive us to bankruptcy. I hated myself for thinking that while Christi was suffering, while we lost a child we'd never meet.

Reggie's voice pulls me back into the present. "Are you married?" he asks.

I blink twice.

He pauses, then asks again, his brow furrowing slightly. "Are you *currently* married?"

I blink twice again.

His upbeat demeanor falters for a second, but he quickly moves on. "Do you have any children?"

I blink twice, my mind flashing back to all six of our kids—how much we love them, how chaotic and beautiful our life together has been.

Reggie gives a small, strained laugh. "Alright, alright. I know blinking twice means 'yes,' Mr. Wright. Just making sure we're on the same page."

Yeah, I know, you idiot, I think. *Now hurry up and teach me how to talk again so I can call you an idiot out loud.*

Reggie rubs his chin thoughtfully, then grins again. "Let's try something even easier. Is your name John?"

I blink twice.

"Do you live in Taylor, Texas?"

I blink once, my first "no" answer.

He pauses, glancing down at something on the clipboard he's holding. "Huh. That's strange. Your driver's license says you do." He reads the address aloud, showing me the license. "407 S. Main, Taylor, Texas."

As I look at the license in his hand, it hits me.

Uh-oh.

I'm not me, but I *am* me. I guess I do live in Taylor, Texas now. My stomach sinks as I close my eyes, overwhelmed by the realization. Poor Reggie. He's just trying to help, but there's no way he's been trained for this. No one would know what to do with something like this.

Reggie stands up, his face softening with understanding. "It's okay," he says quietly. "I get it. You're tired. You've been through a lot more than most people ever will. I'll let you rest for now, but I'll be back. You're going to be talking before you know it, Mr. Wright."

As he leaves the room, I'm left alone with the weight of it all. How do I even begin to explain who I really am? How will I ever tell them the truth?

CHAPTER 13
John Hadley

It's almost Christmas Day. I've been working relentlessly with Reggie on my physical and speech therapy. He's been a good guy, and now, I've got the hang of it—giving him the answers he expects, the ones that Jon Wright should know. The routine feels like second nature now. Wright's body is leaner than mine ever was, and despite everything that's happened, I feel strong. I feel good.

Jon Wright is a year older than me, but in his body, I feel younger, more alive. The guy never smoked, and I was a smoker for years. Still, it's strange—I've been craving a cigarette since the moment I woke up in this hospital. Maybe that's just a habit my mind can't let go of, even though this body has probably never touched one.

It's Christmas morning. I'm not technically ready to be discharged yet, but there's no way I'm staying here. Not when I'm this close to seeing Christi. Nothing is going to keep me from my wife. So, I called a cab, and now I am on my way—heading home to Hutto, Texas. It is only about twenty minutes northeast of Austin, but it feels like a lifetime away.

When the cab pulls up in front of my house, a pang of sadness hits me. The place looks... wrong. There are no Christmas decorations. No lights. No blow-up Santa. It is all bare. Normally, Christi loves the holidays. She usually decorates like crazy—sometimes even before Thanksgiving. I remember her testing the light strands the day before I... died.

"Oh, Christi," I whisper under my breath, feeling the weight of her grief even before I see her.

I step up to the door, my heart racing. What am I going to say? How do I even begin to explain this?

Before I can knock, the door swings open. And there she is.

Her face goes pale when she sees me, and she stumbles backward, clutching her chest. "John?" she breathes, her voice trembling.

I step outside, trying to calm her down. The kids can't see me like this. I don't want to cause a scene. "I know this is... a lot," I say softly. "But please, just give me a few minutes to explain."

Christi shakes her head, disbelief written all over her face. "I know who you are," she says, her voice shaky but firm. "You're John."

"Yes, but I'm not the John you think I am," I say, my heart pounding in my chest. This is it. This is the moment I have been dreading.

But she does not let me finish. "You're John Hadley, my husband," she says, her eyes brimming with tears.

The weight of her words hits me like a punch to the gut. I squeezed her hand, pulling her into a hug, desperate to hold her, to feel her warmth again. She hugs me back, and for a moment, everything feels right. Like it used to be. But then the questions come rushing in.

"How?" she whispers against my chest. "How are you here?"

I pulled back just enough to look into her eyes, searching for the right words. "I don't know how to explain it. But I had to come back. For you. For the kids."

Christi's eyes are wide, filled with a mix of fear and hope. "I saw you," she says, her voice barely a whisper. "In the hospital. You led me to your room. I sat beside you, but the nurse... the doctor... they said it was not you."

I nod, trying to keep my emotions in check. "It was me, Christi. I'm here."

She pulls away slightly, glancing over her shoulder. "Chelsea... I want Chelsea to see you. She needs to see what I see."

I nod again, unsure of what is going to happen but willing to do whatever it takes. Christi calls out to Chelsea, asking her to come to the front porch. A moment later, our daughter appears, her face set in a hard scowl.

She crosses her arms, rolling her eyes. "Yeah, I know who he is," she says, her voice dripping with anger. "He's the man who killed your unborn children's father."

The words hang in the air like a cloud of smoke, thick and suffocating. I feel the blood drain from my face. The accusation hits me harder than I could've ever prepared for. Before I can even process what she's said, everything goes black.

When I come to, I am lying on the porch, looking up at the sky. My body feels heavy, my head pounding. I hear Christi's voice calling for help, and then I see her and Chelsea, both struggling to lift me. I try to help, but my legs feel like lead.

"Luke!" Christi shouts, and moments later, our son appears, strong and capable. He helps carry me into the living room, his eyes wide with concern.

The kids are all gathered around, their faces a mixture of confusion and fear. They want to know who I am, what is happening.

Before I can say anything, I see them—Vince and Campbell, my twin boys. They look just like I remember. Vince is as outgoing as ever, his eyes sparkling with curiosity. Campbell, quieter, more thoughtful, watches me intently. Something in him shifts. He walks over to me, sitting down in my lap as if he has done it a thousand times before.

Tears well up in my eyes as I look at them—my boys. My heart aches with love and relief. I'm here. I am finally here.

Christi stands beside me, her hand on my shoulder. "I know this is... crazy," she says softly. "But it's happening. We will find a way to make this work."

I nod, still holding onto Campbell, feeling the weight of everything that has happened, everything that still needs to be explained to a plethora of people. But for now, for this moment, I am home.

CHAPTER 14
John Hadley

Jon's brother, Michael, just found out I'm in the hospital. The real problem is, Jon Wright's brother is coming to see me, but in Jon Wright's body. I have no idea what this guy is like. Now, I'm stuck nervously waiting for a visit from a brother I know nothing about.

I should not have come back to the hospital after that strange visit with my real family earlier today.

Christi keeps telling me, "We need to be careful. People will not understand why I'm pregnant and suddenly dating someone right after you died."

"I wish we could just tell everyone the truth," I mutter, frustrated. "Who's gonna believe a body snatching story, though? I don't even know if I believe it myself, and I'm the damn body snatcher."

Before she can respond, I hear the door creak open, and Michael walks in. I quickly close my eyes and pretend to be asleep, hoping he'll say something I can use to convince him I'm Jon.

He sits beside me, and after a long pause, I hear him start crying. Sobbing, really, like a little kid.

"My God," I think. "None of my real brothers would cry like this, except maybe Daniel when our football team lost the championship."

Michael keeps talking through his tears, his words barely understandable. He mentions his wife—her name's Shelly—and something about their kids. I try to piece together what he's saying, but all I can focus on is how uncomfortable I feel with a grown man breaking down like this. Still, I listen, knowing I need to keep this act going.

"I'll be back to check on you later, Jon," he finally says, wiping his nose and standing up.

I almost sigh in relief. I can't wait to get out of here before I have to deal with more of this.

But before I can relax, I hear a voice that sends shivers down my spine. It's him. Christi's ex-husband, Royce Madison.

He walks into the room, grinning like he owns the place. "Mr. Madison," he introduces himself with a smug smile. I give him a nod, trying to keep up the facade that I'm Jon Wright and can barely speak.

"I just wanted to check on you, see how you're doing," he says, still grinning. "You know that wreck—well, it was a blessing in disguise."

I can feel my fists clenching under the blankets. "A blessing?" I almost growl, but I keep quiet.

He leans in closer. "I have always loved Christi, you know. And with John out of the picture, I'm gonna win her back."

I am seeing red now. "Over my dead body," I think, though I keep my face neutral.

Trying to keep my voice steady, I say, "You ready to raise John Hadley's twins?"

He freezes. His smile falters, and he stares at me. "Twins? What are you talking about? Christi's not pregnant."

"Oh, but she is. I am talking about the twins she is carrying now. The ones in utero," I say, watching his face for the reaction.

He looks stunned, his mouth opening and closing like a fish out of water. "How... how do you know that?"

I realized I might have gone too far, but I recovered quickly. "Oh, I overheard the nurses talking about it. You know how it is, hospital gossip."

He laughs, but it is forced, his shock is still evident. "Her tubes were tied years ago. There is no way she's pregnant."

"I must've misunderstood," I say with a shrug, playing dumb. "Maybe I am still loopy from all these meds. For all I know, the Queen of England's having twins."

He chuckles, but I can see the doubt in his eyes. He excuses himself, mumbling something about needing to get going. I watch him leave, feeling the tension in my shoulders ease.

I grabbed the phone and called Christi. "You won't believe who just paid me a visit," I tell her, filling her in on everything Royce said.

"He actually said that?" she asks, shocked. "Do not worry, I'm not going anywhere near him. I will make sure to keep my distance."

"Good," I reply, feeling a sense of relief. "By the way, Jon's brother Michael came by earlier."

"Oh?" she says. "I knew a Michael Wright in school back in Tyler. We were actually pretty close."

"Really?" I ask, trying to keep my voice neutral.

She laughs softly. "Yeah, I had the biggest crush on him back then. We even made out in a closet once during a game of truth or dare."

My blood boils. "You're kidding," I mutter under my breath. "Please tell me it's not the same guy."

She laughs again, not sensing my frustration. "It is probably the same guy, but you never know. I know he also had a brother whose name is Jon."

I clench my fists again, trying to keep my cool. "First, his brother ruins my life, then he ruins my Christmas, and now I find out this guy made out with my wife?"

Christi must sense my mood shift because she quickly changes the subject. "We need to go to Jon's house soon, figure out more about his life. You have got to learn how to live as him, right?"

I sigh, my frustration is still simmering. "Yeah, I guess you are right. But I have only ever met the guy at the crossroads of life and death. How do I pretend to be someone I barely know?"

CHAPTER 15

A week later—or technically, a year later, because today is January 1, 2013—I am finally released from the hospital. Michael comes to pick me up and take me home, but Jon Wright's house is not the house I want to see. I brace myself, knowing that I will have to excuse my unfamiliarity with things by claiming amnesia if I'm going to convince this man's brother that I am, in fact, Jon Wright.

As we drive along Highway 79, I catch sight of the accident site. Neon-colored spray paint marks the pavement, highlighting the point of impact and what must be my skid marks. Michael glances over at me, following my gaze.

"Is that where it happened?" he asks.

I nod and mutter, "Yeah." My voice is flat, hollow. It is all I can manage.

We pulled into a convenience store, and I stepped inside to grab a six-pack of Miller Lite. As I place it on the counter, I catch Michael's surprised expression out of the corner of my eye. He eyes the beer and then looks at me, puzzled.

"I thought you hated beer," he says, his voice light but questioning.

I shrug, playing off the confusion. "The wreck's got my head all messed up," I explain. "I don't even know what I like anymore."

He gives me a half-smile, clearly unconvinced but willing to let it slide. "Well, I guess I better grab a six-pack for myself then," he says with a laugh, heading back into the store.

Once we are at Jon's house, I get my first real look at my new home. It is a lovely place—a three-bedroom house, fully paid off. That is more than I can say for the one I had. We settle on the back porch with our beers, and I brace myself for what I know is coming.

"So," Michael says, cracking open a can. "Tell me everything. I want all the sorted details."

I take a long swig, feeling the buzz start to hit. Maybe it's the alcohol, maybe it's the exhaustion, but I start telling him the truth. I tell him everything.

At first, Michael just laughs, shaking his head like I am telling him some kind of elaborate joke. "Man, you're crazy," he says between laughs. "You need to head back to the hospital."

The mood shifts, his laughter killing whatever buzz I had. Realizing I have gone too far, I quickly changed course. "Nah, I am just messing with you. I must have dozed off at the wheel and hit John Hadley's car head-on," I say with a shrug, trying to make it sound casual.

Michael sighs, rubbing the back of his neck. "Yeah, well, be more careful. I gotta head back to Dallas tomorrow," he says, his voice now tinged with exhaustion.

We ended up talking the rest of the night, mostly about football—something Jon Wright apparently didn't care much for. But Michael does not seem to mind. We are both buzzed, and he laughs at my stories, even though I've never been more serious. It feels oddly comforting. He is funny, too, cracking jokes that make me feel like we've known each other forever.

By the end of the night, I started wondering if I have been missing something with my own brothers. Maybe we weren't as close as we could've been.

Turns out, Michael is a financial analyst, just like Jon. They even work for the same company, though Michael's based in Dallas. He confides in me that he is miserable in his marriage, staying with his wife only for the sake of the kids. "I can't lose them," he says, taking a swig of beer. "Most men know that divorce means less time with your kids. The maternal enemy gets the upper hand."

His words hit me harder than I expected, and I feel a pang of sympathy. I casually ask, "Did we go to high school in Tyler?"

"Yeah," Michael says, frowning slightly. "You really are having some memory issues after this accident. We went to Robert E. Lee High School in Tyler, Texas."

"Do you remember a girl named Christi Lynn Zimmer?" I ask, trying to keep my voice steady.

He looks at me, eyebrows raised, and then nods. "Yeah, I remember her. I was in love with her back in high school. She was something else. But I heard she got pregnant and moved away." He pauses. "Why do you ask?"

I keep my expression neutral, pretending it's no big deal. "I was searching John Hadley online, and I saw a picture of him with his wife, Christi. She looked familiar, but I was not sure if I was remembering her from school."

Michael laughs softly. "Small world," he says. But there is a flicker of recognition in his eyes, and I can tell he's piecing things together.

Before we know it, it is 3 a.m., and we both decide to call it a night. I stumble into the guest room—my room now, I guess—and crash onto the bed. As I close my eyes, I cannot help but think that this bed is way too comfortable for a guy who just had his entire life flipped upside down.

CHAPTER 16

I wake up to a knock at the door. Peering at the clock, I see it is already 10 a.m. Today was supposed to be Jon Wright's first day back at work, and I have already blew that. Michael needed to leave early in the morning too, but apparently, he's still asleep. Before I can process more, I hear footsteps moving quickly through the house. Michael runs into the living room, clearly in a hurry, his face a mixture of confusion and urgency. I open the front door, and standing there is Christi. The sight of her takes my breath away. I melted just seeing her beautiful face. "Christi..." I whisper, but my voice fails me, too full of emotion.

Without hesitation, I invite her in, and the second she steps inside, she pulls me into a tight hug. Her warmth is all I need in this world. Before I know it, she leans in and kisses me, softly but with the kind of passion that says everything words cannot.

"Ahem," Michael coughs, breaking the moment as he clears his throat loudly.

Christi jumps, startled by his presence, pulling away from me in a quick motion.

"Oh!" she gasps, her hand flying to her chest. "I didn't realize anyone else was here."

I awkwardly gesture between them.

"Christi, this is Michael... Jon Wright's brother."

Michael stands there, his gaze bouncing between us, eyebrows knitted together in confusion. I can almost see the gears turning in his head. His silence is unnerving, and I can tell he is processing all of this in real time—probably trying to make sense of why his brother is kissing this woman the day after his release from the hospital.

Finally, he clears his throat again, this time with something more to say. His voice is calm but filled with disbelief.

"You really are John Hadley, aren't you?"

His words land like a hammer. Christi and I stand there frozen, speechless. There it is, the unthinkable notion said aloud. How does anyone process a thing like this? Even I struggle to believe it sometimes.

"Michael…" I begin, unsure how to approach the truth yet again. He's already heard it once, but seeing us together must've pushed him into believing it.

I glance at Christi for support, but she looks just as unsure. There is a long pause before Michael speaks again, his eyes misting over with the weight of it all.

"So... you saw Jon and Debbie?" he asks, his voice cracking as he speaks her name.

I nod slowly, not trusting my voice to remain steady. The mention of Jon and Debbie tugs at him hard. It is written all over his face.

"Yeah," I manage to say softly, but my voice does not come out right. The memories of what happened flood back.

Michael wipes his eyes, but the tears keep coming. His next question is directed at Christi.

"How do you know this man is your husband?" he asks, his tone less accusatory and more curious now.

She pauses, her eyes glistening with unshed tears, as she recounts her experience.

"I know what I saw. I saw *him*," she says firmly, squeezing my hand.

Her words feel surreal, but I trust her more than anyone else in the world. I do not remember leading her to my body, but if she says it happened, then it did. There is so much I don't remember from those days—physically and spiritually exhausted doesn't even begin to cover it. It's as though pieces of me got left behind in the wreckage.

Michael's tears return as he listens, but this time, there is a hint of something else there—comfort, maybe? He sniffles and asks, "What does it all mean? For us? For those of us still here?"

His question lingers heavily in the air, and Christi and I exchange glances. The truth is, we do not know. None of us knows how this is going to play out.

"We don't have all the answers, Michael," I admit. "We are still trying to figure it all out. I am just... trying to live as Jon Wright."

He nods slowly, absorbing my words.

"You are right. We need to be careful who we tell. No one is going to believe this... not without thinking we're all insane."

Christi nods in agreement, her voice quieter now.

"We agree, Michael. But how do we go on pretending? He's Jon Wright now, but he does not know the first thing about his job, or his life..."

Michael gives a deep sigh, as though the weight of the world just settled onto his shoulders.

"You're right. We need to figure out a way for you to keep living this life. I will help in any way I can."

He gets to his feet and walks toward the door but turns back before stepping outside.

"We're brothers, you know."

His words feel like a balm to my soul. I smile, grateful for the acceptance. At least two people in this world believe me, and that is more than I could've hoped for.

"Yeah, we are," I reply, my voice thick with emotion.

Michael heads down the driveway, off to face his three-and-a-half-hour drive back to Dallas. I stand in the doorway, watching him go, imagining the thoughts running through his head. He has got a lot to process.

I really like this new brother of mine. I just wish it did not have to happen like this—with so much loss and confusion. But, for now, we have to focus on what comes next. The challenge is learning to live Jon Wright's life without losing mine.

CHAPTER 17

Christi and I stepped into Jon Wright's empty home, the silence wrapping around us like a warm blanket. With six children, we were rarely alone, and the quiet felt both freeing and unsettling. I glanced into her baby blue eyes, searching for a hint of what she was feeling.

"Wow, it's really quiet in here," I said, breaking the silence.

Christi smiled softly. "Yeah, too quiet, right?"

I leaned closer, feeling a surge of affection. "Come here." I pulled her into a kiss, my hands gently caressing her face and running through her hair. As the kiss deepened, I felt a mix of passion and uncertainty. "Let's check out the master bedroom."

I took her hand and led her into the spacious room, laying her down on the King Size bed. "This is nice," I said, looking around.

"It is," she replied, her voice barely above a whisper.

I lifted her shirt, kissing a path from her neck down to her chest, eventually resting my lips on her pregnant belly. I glanced up, catching her smile, but then I felt a sudden tension in the air as I started to pull off her black leggings.

"Wait," she said, stopping me. Her voice was firm, yet there was a flicker of hesitation in her eyes.

I felt a pang of confusion. "What's wrong?"

"I—I just can't," she stammered, looking away. "It feels wrong."

Hurt washed over me, but I tried to mask it. "You don't have to explain."

"I'm sorry," she said, her voice shaky.

"This is awkward for both of us," I replied, trying to maintain some semblance of calm. "Can you tell me what you're thinking?"

She took a deep breath, her gaze piercing through mine. "It does not feel right. You are in his body, and I can't shake that feeling."

I nodded, letting her words settle in the space between us. "Okay, let's change the subject. What do you think about getting a new car?"

Her brows furrowed slightly, and she shifted, as if the weight of our conversation still lingered. "Yeah, we definitely need to figure that out. Jon's car… it is gone now."

As we sifted through Jon's desk, I uncovered a pile of bank statements and pay stubs. "Look at this," I said, holding up his social security card. "He's got enough money to buy a car outright if he wants to."

Christi peered over my shoulder, finding an unopened bank statement. "Wow, Jon had more than enough. We should head to that Ford dealership in Hutto."

"I've always wanted a truck," I admitted, excitement bubbling up as we headed to the dealership.

Once there, I spotted a fully loaded black F150 with leather seats. "This is it!" I exclaimed, my heart racing at the sight of it.

"It looks perfect for you," Christi said, a smile lighting up her face.

"Perfect? It's incredible! I could never have afforded this back when I was John Hadley with six kids," I said, grinning from ear to ear. "But with Jon's salary, we can make it work."

As I signed the paperwork, the weight of Jon's life pressed down on me. "I pulled away from the dealership, grinning like a kid on Christmas morning," I said, feeling a rush of accomplishment.

Christi followed me to Jon's house in Taylor, and we stopped at a Chinese restaurant.

As we walked in, a young Asian woman greeted me with enthusiasm. "Mr. Wright! It is so good to see you!"

I smiled, but confusion washed over me. "Uh, yeah… good to see you too?"

Christi laughed lightly. "It is strange, isn't it? People know you, but you do not recognize them."

"Yeah, it feels surreal," I admitted, placing our to-go order. "Let's get back to Jon's place."

Once we arrived, the conversation shifted to finances, living arrangements, and sleeping arrangements. "So, while your kids are with your ex and mine with their mom for the break, what do you think about spending the night here?" Christi nodded with a yes.

"I'd love that," she said. The warmth of her presence comforting.

While Christi took a bubble bath in the large Jacuzzi tub, I sat on the edge, washing her back gently. "You know, this feels nice," I said, trying to ease the tension.

"Yeah, it does," she replied, though I noticed her slightly shy away from me.

After her bath, she pulled a t-shirt from Jon's closet. My stomach twisted at the sight of her wearing another man's clothes. "You look… good," I said, forcing a smile as she climbed into bed beside me.

"Thanks," she murmured, turning to her side as I spooned her, placing my hand gently on her belly. "So, what are we going to name these little invaders?" I asked, my voice playful.

She chuckled softly. "I haven't really thought about it yet."

"I think we should pick gender-neutral names," I suggested, a spark of excitement igniting in me. "How about Blake for one?"

Her brow furrowed in thought. "I was leaning towards names starting with A and B for baby A and baby B. I like Blake, though. It has a nice ring to it."

"Great! We have some time to decide," I said, feeling the warmth of her presence.

"When's your next doctor's appointment?" I asked, shifting the topic.

"It's in a few weeks," she replied, looking a bit anxious. "But I don't think you should come with me."

"Why not?" I pressed, puzzled.

"Because… Jon Wright is not my husband. What would Dr. Andrews think if I brought a strange man with me?" she said, her voice edged with frustration.

"I don't care what he thinks," I insisted, my tone firm.

Her eyes flashed with anger. "Well, I do! It is too soon after Jon's accident!"

"Christi, this is not about him! It is about us," I replied, my frustration bubbling over.

Out of nowhere, she blurted, "Goodnight!"

"Wait, Christi, can I have a kiss? You promised me you would always kiss me goodnight."

"No, I promised my husband that," she shot back, her tone sharp.

"So, I'm not your husband?" I challenged, feeling the sting of her words.

"You know what I mean!" she snapped, her emotions boiling.

"No, Christi, I don't!" I said, desperation creeping into my voice. "We're here together."

"This is too much. It is too hard to deal with. Maybe I should just go home," she said, tears glistening in her eyes.

"Fine. Go home then. Go back to your perfect life without me," I spat, my heart racing. "Call your ex and ask him to help you raise your twins while you're at it!"

"Really, John? My twins?" she retorted, hurt flashing across her face.

"No, your dead husband's twins!" I shot back, my anger spilling over.

She glared at me, her voice trembling. "I'm leaving."

I watched as Christi, my wife with our unborn twins, walked out to her car. A feeling of emptiness washed over me, a hollow ache deep within. I felt like I was dying all over again, but what could I do?

CHAPTER 18
Christi

66Why am I crying like this?" I muttered to myself. Tears streamed down my face as I walked into the house, feeling helpless against the flood of emotions, wiping away the streaks of mascara running down my cheeks. "I hate these pregnancy hormones."

I had prayed for John to come back to me, but not like this—not in someone else's body. Our children would not understand, and the thought of hurting them weighed heavily on me. They had already been through so much.

As I stepped inside, Chelsea noticed my face immediately.

"Mom, what's wrong?" she asked, her voice filled with concern.

I forced a smile and waved it off. "It is just the pregnancy... I am being emotional. I miss John," I admitted, my voice barely above a whisper.

Chelsea offered a sympathetic smile. "Well, you've got me, at least."

Her words warmed my heart, and I nodded. "Yeah, I know. We are more like sisters than mother and daughter sometimes, aren't we?"

She grinned. "Always."

Just then, my phone buzzed in my pocket—John was calling. I stared at the screen, but I could not bring myself to answer. What would I even say? How could I talk to my dead husband who now walked around in someone else's skin? For the first time in my life, I was at a complete loss for words.

"I can't do this right now," I whispered to myself, putting the phone back in my pocket.

If I had answered, maybe things wouldn't have spiraled the way they did. But instead, I found myself standing frozen as the front door swung open. John walked through, and I watched as Chelsea's face turned from confusion to horror.

Her scream cut through the silence.

John rushed over to me, pulling me into his arms. "It's okay," he whispered, his voice soothing. "I know this is hard... it is not fair. But this is our second chance. We cannot take this for granted. I love you, and I am not leaving you again."

Chelsea stared at us, her eyes wide with disbelief. "Who... who are you? What are you?" Her voice trembled, fear and confusion mixing together.

John glanced at her with a soft smile. "I am the guy who owes you twenty bucks. Do not think I've forgotten. And you are the girl who walked on my back before I left on December 3rd."

Chelsea's tear-filled eyes blinked in shock. Then, suddenly, she let out a sob. But before I could comfort her, she ran toward John and threw her arms around him, hugging him tightly.

"I knew you wanted to lose weight, but this is extreme!" she cried, her voice muffled by her tears.

We all burst into laughter, the tension easing just a little. "You and John could have your own comedy show, you know that?" I teased, wiping the last of my tears.

"Timing is everything," Chelsea shot back, still sniffling, but her smile was genuine.

I glanced at the clock and sighed. "It's late, maybe we should all get some sleep."

Chelsea shook her head firmly. "No way! I need to understand all of this! How did this even happen?"

John chuckled. "Well, it's a long story."

We all settled onto the massive sectional couch, and John began explaining everything—about the accident, Jon Wright, and his wife Debbie. I must have dozed off somewhere in the middle of it because the next thing I knew, I was yawning and blinking at the soft light in the room.

The house was still dim, but the lights from the kitchen cast a soft glow. I squinted, trying to adjust my eyes, and saw John and Chelsea still talking, their laughter filling the air. Seeing them so full of joy again made my heart swell.

Before I could say anything, John scooped me up into his arms. "Whoa, what are you doing?" I laughed.

"I'm carrying my wife to bed," he said, grinning. "Won't be able to do this in a few months."

I chuckled. "I am perfectly capable of walking, you know. It is safer that way!"

He carried me into the bedroom and laid me down on the bed, gently kissing my forehead. "This feels so right," he murmured, climbing into bed next to me.

I could not help but smile. "Yeah, it does."

The bed felt familiar—our usual sides, the soft sheets, the downy comforter. But there was something about having him next to me again, in our bed, that made everything feel surreal. I turned toward him and kissed him softly.

He returned the kiss, but there was something different in the way his lips met mine—something deeper, more urgent. The kiss grew, turning from something tender into a passionate wave that left me breathless.

John's hands roamed my body, his touch slow, deliberate. He kissed every inch of my skin, paying special attention to certain areas, his lips and hands reverent and tender. It felt like we were rediscovering each other, our connection more intense than it had ever been before.

As we made love, the feeling of desperation lingered between us, like we were racing against time, like every touch mattered more than it ever had. Tears welled in his eyes as he looked down at me, his emotions raw and unfiltered.

"I'm so thankful for this moment," he whispered, his voice cracking.

I felt my own tears spilling over, a torrent of emotions overwhelming me. "Me too," I choked out.

We collapsed together afterward, exhausted but content. I rested my head on his chest, the steady rise and fall of his breath calming me.

It was then I noticed it—his chest was smooth, hairless. My John always had a hairy chest. I used to love running my fingers through it, but now, Jon Wright's body felt foreign, unfamiliar.

I did not mind it, not really. But it was another reminder that the man lying next to me was both my husband... and not.

CHAPTER 19

I wake, almost startled to see my husband staring at me. His gaze is warm, and I cannot help but smile before leaning in to kiss him. Today is January 3, 2013. It has been a month since the accident, and the kids will be home in a few days— Sunday, January 6th. I want to spend as much time with John as I can before then.

John cannot be here when Luke, Jan, and Emily come home. Luke is seventeen now, and though he was calm on Christmas morning when he saw Jon Wright's body, I'm not sure he will be as understanding this time. He is a boxer, and well, he might not take kindly to "Jon" being around again. As for Jan and Emily, they are only ten and seven. They are too young to know that Jon Wright is responsible for John's "death," and it's too soon for them to see me with another man—even if that man is really their stepdad. They have already lost him once.

I glance at John, who is moving about the kitchen, making breakfast. He has been so sweet since he came back, and I can tell he's trying to be the perfect husband, especially after everything that's happened.

"What're you making?" I ask, leaning forward on the granite kitchen island, one of my favorite spots in the house.

"Just some eggs and bacon," he says, cracking another egg into the pan with a soft sizzle. "Figured you could use a good breakfast."

I smile, but the thought of food makes my stomach turn. Pregnancy nausea hits me hard, and everything smells so strong. The eggs, the bacon, even the soap from the dishes we washed earlier.

"I appreciate it, but I don't know if I can handle the smell of eggs right now," I admit, my hand instinctively resting on my belly.

John turns to me with a soft chuckle. "Smells bothering you again?"

I nod, scrunching my nose. "Yeah, I think the babies and I are boycotting breakfast."

His phone rings, cutting through our conversation. I glance at the screen as he picks it up. The caller ID flashes *Michael*. John's face changes as soon as he answers, his brow furrowing. He listens intently, and I can tell something is wrong.

"Yes, of course," John says after a moment, his voice serious.

When he hangs up, I look at him, curious. "What was that about? Is everything okay?"

He hesitates for a second, then sighs. "Michael's coming to stay with me for a while. His wife… she left him for another man."

"Oh, no," I say, my heart sinking. "That's awful."

John nods, leaning against the counter. "Yeah, it is. But, you know, I think it might be good. He will have someone to talk to, and so will I."

I can see it in his eyes—he is thinking about how lonely it's going to be when I'm not around. And as much as it hurts, I know it's true. He will need someone when I cannot be there.

"Michael wants to transfer to Austin," John continues. "He asked if he and his boys could stay with me until he finds a place."

I blink, surprised. "With you?"

"Yeah, I said yes. I mean, I could not say no."

I nod slowly. "Of course, I understand. It might be good for you, having someone around."

He comes up behind me, wrapping his arms around my waist and resting his chin on my shoulder. "How are you feeling?" he asks softly, rubbing my belly. "Are you and the babies hungry?"

"I'm hungry," I say, leaning into him, "but I don't know what I can eat that won't make me sick."

As if on cue, my phone rings from the other room. A chill runs down my spine, a feeling I cannot quite shake. I walked over to check the caller ID and see it is my mother-in-law, Pam.

I answer, my voice hesitant. "Hello?"

The sound of Pam's sobs hits me immediately. "Pam? What is wrong?" I ask, my heart pounding.

"Jean… Jean is dead," Pam chokes out through her tears. "She… she went out drinking, and… on her way to the babysitter's house, she lost control of the car."

I feel the blood drain from my face. "Oh, no… Oh, Pam, I'm so sorry…"

"They found her dead at the scene," Pam continues, her voice breaking. "The car flipped, and… they found beer cans, a meth pipe… the boys are still at the sitter's house. We need to get them."

I close my eyes, trying to process what I am hearing. Jean is gone, and now her boys are without their mother. My heart aches for them, for Pam, for everyone involved.

"Pam, we'll get the boys," I manage to say, my voice shaking. "We'll take care of them."

John, sensing my distress, comes up behind me and places his hand on my back. I feel his steady presence, and it is enough to keep me grounded, for now. I turn to him, and in that moment, I realize—no matter what happens, we will get through this. Together.

CHAPTER 20

Pam asks me if I can pick the boys up from the sitter and bring them to my house until she can get to Austin. I do not hesitate for a second. "Of course," I tell her, my voice steady despite the swirl of emotions inside. These sweet boys have already lost their father a month ago—now their mother too? My heart aches for them, and even though I am upset with Jean, I try to focus on what the boys need right now.

I hang up and turn to Jon. "Get dressed quickly," I say, already moving to grab my things.

Jon looks at me with concern. "What happened?"

I explain what Pam just shared with me, watching as John's face shifts from confusion to shock, then anger. He sits down heavily on the edge of the bed, his hands running through his hair. I know his hurt is not for Jean—there was no love lost between them after their messy divorce—but for the boys. They've been through so much, and now this.

"She was using drugs, John," I say softly, trying to break the silence. "I had no idea."

John shakes his head, his voice low and rough. "I knew she had issues... but I never thought it was this bad."

We do not say much else as we drive to Becky's house. She has been the boys' sitter for about a year, and when we arrive, I can see them through the

63

window, sitting at the kitchen table, sipping hot chocolate. They have no idea their lives are about to be turned upside down again.

Becky opens the door before we even knock. She looks grim but tries to force a smile. "They don't know anything yet," she whispers. "I... I didn't know how to tell them."

I nod, my throat tight as I step inside. The boys look up, smiling when they see us. Campbell, the younger twin, runs straight to John, his little arms wrapping around his leg. Vince, the older twin, is more reserved, walks toward me. I pulled him into a tight hug, squeezing so hard I accidentally hurt him.

"Ouch," he mumbles, and I loosen my grip, kissing his forehead.

John, who has been holding back his emotions, suddenly breaks down. He kneels in front of Vince, his eyes red, and asks softly, "Can I get a hug too, buddy?"

Vince hesitates for a moment before nodding. "Okay, Daddy."

John glances at me in disbelief. I am stunned too. We have suspected Campbell might recognize John, but Vince? He has been so indifferent. It is as if he knew all along but didn't want to believe it.

I kneel down beside the boys. "Do you know who this is?" I ask gently, looking between them.

Both boys nod solemnly. "Mommy came to us in a dream last night," Campbell says quietly. "She told us he's our dad, even though he looks different."

My breath catches in my throat. "She... she did?"

Vince nods. "She said she's in heaven now, but that we'll see her again."

I glance at John, my mind racing. I have always believed in miracles, in the possibility of an afterlife. But hearing the boys talk so calmly about Jean visiting them, about her telling them the truth—it is overwhelming. I find myself blinking back tears.

John, however, seems more grounded. He gathers the boys, holding them close, as if trying to absorb their pain. "Your mom loves you both so much," he whispers. "She's watching over you. Always."

The boys seem at peace with that, as if their pure innocence shields them from the full gravity of the situation. They do not cry. They do not seem devastated. It is almost as if they understand something we adults can't.

We take the boys back to our house, the weight of what just happened settling in. I know Pam will be here soon, and I am dreading the moment she sees John. The boys stick to him like glue, and I know he will not be able to leave before Pam arrives. It is inevitable.

When Pam finally knocks on the door, she does not even wait for us to answer. She steps inside, her eyes immediately falling on John, who is sitting on the couch with Campbell on his lap.

For a split second, I think she is going to handle it well. But then her face turns white, and before any of us can react, she screams.

The boys flinch, but John remains calm. "Go upstairs, guys," he says gently. "Play your Wii for a bit."

The boys hesitate but do as they are told, their footsteps echoing up the stairs as they leave the room. Pam, meanwhile, is staring at John, her hands shaking, her lips moving as if she is trying to form words.

Then, without warning, she passes out.

I rush to her side, but John is already there. He lifts her carefully, laying her down on the couch. "Get me a wet washcloth," he says over his shoulder, and I hurry to the bathroom, grabbing one from the cabinet. When I return, John gently pats Pam's face with the cool cloth, and after a few moments, her eyes flutter open.

She looks around, confused. "John?" she mumbles, her voice hoarse.

I kneeled beside her. "Pam, are you okay?"

She nods weakly, but her eyes are still glued to John. I can see her mind working, trying to make sense of the impossible. She sits up slowly, her voice shaking as she says, "Is it really you?"

John nods. "It's me, Mom."

Pam's eyes well up with tears. "Why... why didn't you tell me?" she asks, looking at me accusingly.

"I tried," I say softly. "But no one believed me. I didn't want to... to sound crazy."

Pam laughs, but it is a shaky, awkward sound. "Well, I guess we're all a little crazy now, aren't we?"

She reaches out, and John pulls her into a hug. She clings to him, sobbing quietly into his shoulder. After a few moments, she pulls back, wiping her eyes. "You have to call your father," she says, her voice stronger now.

John shakes his head. "I don't think that's a good idea."

Pam sighs, understanding but still struggling with the reality of the situation. "I know. But... it just feels like we should."

The conversation drifts, and I realize how hungry I am. I have not eaten all day, and I'm starting to feel lightheaded. I excuse myself, heading to the kitchen. Oddly, I am craving hotdogs. I pull one from the fridge and start preparing a plate.

As I cook, I can hear Pam questioning John in the living room, asking him things only he would know. She is putting him to the test, still trying to wrap her mind around the impossible. I cannot blame her. Sometimes, I doubt it myself.

But as I hear John answering each question, I cannot help but smile. No matter how unbelievable it is, this man—this impossible miracle—is my husband. And somehow, that is all that matters.

CHAPTER 21

Pam is legally the next of kin to take care of Vince and Campbell, but she knows the boys need to be with John, even if it is John 2.0. John has no legal standing to parent the boys, because in the eyes of the court, he is Jon Wright. Vince and Campbell, however, tell Pam about their celestial visit from Jean the other night. These events are incredible on their own, but when you have multiple strange things happening all at once, it is a lot to digest for anyone.

Pam suggests reaching out to Jean's sister about the funeral arrangements. Jean's parents are deceased, and her sister is the only family member left to oversee the service. I propose a memorial service for Jean, knowing her sister is not wealthy and there's not a large family to attend. Ultimately, Jean's sister will make the final decision. Pam calls her, and I hear her start to cry on the phone.

While Pam is on the call, Michael arrives at our house with his two children. I pull him aside and ask, "Do you have a few minutes to talk?"

He nods, and I can tell he is burdened. "It's not easy for me," he admits, the intensity of his words catching me off guard. "I never wanted to get a divorce."

I tread carefully, knowing he is still raw from his wife's betrayal. "Do you... want to know why?"

Michael stares at me for a second, contemplating. "No, it does not matter anymore. I just cannot do it. The betrayal is too much."

I nod, respecting his space. "John is going to need companionship. Maybe you two can lean on each other during this," I offer, trying to lighten the mood. A small smile breaks on his face, as if he is just realizing that he might be exactly what John needs right now.

We rejoin everyone in the living room, discussing plans—who is going where, and with whom. The day feels heavier, colder, as if January itself is in sync with our emotions. Texas does not have many frigid days, but today is certainly one of them.

John has a follow-up appointment with Dr. Stark today. He is scheduled for an MRI to check for further hemorrhaging and to monitor the hematomas that still need time to heal. We walk across the street to the hospital. It is only a short walk, but I know it'll be good for John to move around a bit.

At the front desk of the radiology center, the nurse pulls up John's information. Dr. Stark has already sent over the orders. John heads to the back for his MRI while I sit in the waiting room, fighting the urge to go with him. Letting him out of my sight, even for a few minutes, feels almost impossible. He is anxious about the results, but John never shares his worries outright. I can feel the weight of them, though, even if he will not admit it.

As I sit there, waiting, my mind drifts to my own doctor's appointment next week. I suspect John will want to come along. WE had a light disagreement about this, but I am grateful for his presence, even if it adds to the complexity of everything going on. I know it will be awkward at the appointment.

I am startled by my thoughts when I see John walking towards me. He smiles when our eyes meet, and I cannot help but smile back.

"I love you," he says simply.

"I love you too."

We walk out hand-in-hand, and as we reach the parking lot, I ask, "You're coming with me to my appointment, right?"

"Of course," he replies, his voice firm, reassuring.

We decide to grab lunch at our favorite little Mexican restaurant. John does not usually rave about Mexican food in this area, but we've always liked this particular spot. As we sit down, memories flood back. The last time I was here, it was with Chelsea, and I had the oddest urge to order cheese enchiladas for John. At the time, Chelsea chided me for speaking aloud about it, but now, I realize I was sensing him. I felt his presence back then, even though I had not seen him yet. Somehow, deep down, I knew we had unfinished business—after all, we are about to have two babies together.

After lunch, we headed to Jon Wright's house. Michael and his kids are already there. He greets us with a hug, and I feel an unexpected warmth from him as his arms wrap around me.

"Thanks for letting us stay here," he says to John, his voice filled with gratitude.

As Michael releases me from the hug, I feel a familiar tingle. Old memories resurface, ones I have not thought about in years. I never truly got over Michael. If I had not met Chelsea and Luke's father, I wonder if Michael and I would've been high school sweethearts. That thought lingers longer than I expected as we walk inside.

CHAPTER 22

The next few days were a whirlwind of time spent with John. We went to the movies, out to dinner, and took long walks, savoring the moments we had together. We talked about everything—conversations we had left unsaid before the accident, dreams we had buried in the rush of life. We spoke of our hopes for the future, how we might finally make them a reality. Buying a house in the country had always been one of our dreams, something we used to talk about before everything changed. Now, with the settlement from the accident, I will finally have the funds to make that happen—a bittersweet gift.

Sunday arrived too soon. It was time for Luke, Jan, and Emily to return home. I missed them dearly, but I would miss John's presence beside me even more. I had grown used to waking up with him next to me again, even if his body was Jon's. John had to return to work now, and I worried. He had no experience with Jon's job as a financial analyst. How could he possibly step into that role? But John was adaptive, always quick to learn. He had Michael help him too, which reassured me. With Michael having transferred to Austin, he would be by John's side, ready to assist him until he found his footing.

It was Wednesday night, and my OBGYN appointment was scheduled for the next morning. I picked up my phone and called John. "Hey, will you pick me up for my appointment tomorrow?" I asked. "Of course," he replied, his voice warm and reassuring.

We both said "I love you" at the same time, our connection undeniable, despite everything. "Bye," I whispered softly.

"Bye," he echoed, and I closed my eyes, finally allowing myself to drift into much-needed sleep.

The next morning, John arrived in a shiny new truck, excitement radiating from him. As I climbed in, he could not wait to tell me about his new job. He was adjusting well, even enjoying the work. Michael had the cubicle next to his, and in the brief time since starting, they had become remarkably close—like brothers, really. John told me how much they enjoyed going to lunch together, talking about life, and sharing stories. It was comforting to know John had someone like Michael by his side during this confusing time.

CHAPTER 23

❝❝Here we are," I say that to break the ice.

Anxiousness courses through me, and a wave of nausea rises in my throat. I am nervous about being in the same room with Jon Wright's body. It is a situation that could easily be misunderstood; people might not comprehend what I'm doing with the man responsible for John's death. But John does not care what anyone thinks.

Dr. Andrews enters, tall and handsome in his scrubs and boots. He listens for heartbeats using the portable Doppler machine. Only one heartbeat resonates through the device. My stomach sinks as he tells me not to worry, but that is all I can do. He suggests we do another sonogram and escorts us into a different room.

John sits beside the ultrasound table as I lie down. Dr. Andrews applies the cold gel to my belly, his expression focused. After a tense moment, he finds both babies and their heartbeats. Tears begin to stream down John's face.

Dr. Andrews notices and quickly tries to look away, confusion flickering across his features. He must feel bewildered by the dynamic between us.

Later that night, something jolted me awake from a deep sleep. I sense I have had a bad dream, but the details escape me. I get up to check on the children. They are all sound asleep—Vince and Campbell are staying here, and a wave of peace washes over me. Yet, I cannot shake the feeling that this tranquility is temporary. Pam has agreed to temporarily relinquish her legal guardianship to me, allowing the boys to continue living in this house. This ensures they can see John and grow up with the new babies.

Chelsea's 19th birthday is approaching, just a week after my wedding anniversary. John and I plan a quiet celebration, but it feels strange to celebrate at all. This is our new normal, and it will take some getting used to. To infuse some joy into our lives, I want to do something special for Chelsea.

I plan a short getaway to Port Aransas, Texas, coinciding with Chelsea's birthday. The beach weather is surprisingly warm for late February. While the water remains cold, the beach and the breeze are invigorating. I wish John could be here with us, but we enjoy our time together, singing happy birthday and indulging in a big cake for Chelsea.

In the days that follow, Jan's birthday, Emily's birthday, and Vance and Campbell's birthday all loom on the horizon. With back-to-back celebrations, my schedule becomes overwhelming, and the expenses add up.

To simplify things, I decided to combine the younger children's birthdays into a pool party at our new house. I have purchased ten acres with a newly built home that features a gorgeous swimming pool. I spared little expense on the pool—it is large, complete with a waterfall, and I had a screened shelter built around it to keep unwanted critters at bay. My favorite feature is the fiber optic lighting for nighttime swims; they promise to be fun and relaxing. We need more moments like that!

The kids are excited about the new house and the pool. I have invited John's entire family and a plethora of friends to the party, along with two rented bouncy houses. I hope the gathering will be a momentous success, and I pray that no one will question Jon Wright's presence. He can remain in the shadows, quietly supporting the kids. Michael and his children will also be there, and he offered to help with both setup and cleanup. I'm easily winded these days, so his support is greatly appreciated. The party is only days away.

CHAPTER 24

I keep waking up in the middle of the night, the same dream haunting me over and over. There is this overwhelming sense of doom, like something terrible is about to happen. I am always in this dark room, stumbling around, feeling the walls, trying to find a door or a light switch. And every time, Michael is there. He saves me from whatever it is that is lurking, waiting to happen.

But I have not told John about the dreams. How would he feel if he knew another man was showing up in my dreams every night? The last thing I want is to upset him or make him think something is wrong with me.

I try to shake it off. I have a doctor's appointment today. "We should know the sex of the babies by the end of this visit," I remind myself, excitement bubbling up. It feels like a good excuse to go shopping. I get out of bed and help the younger kids get ready for the day. Luke's already left for school, and I quickly gather the others, take them to school, and head back to the house to wait for John.

He is taking me to the doctor's office today. We both want to see the sonogram. It is funny—John would have never been this excited about a sonogram. But now, it is different. He should not even be here for this one, and that is what makes today special.

When John arrived early, I smiled at him, relieved. "You ready?" I ask.

"Of course, let's go meet our little ones," he says, his grin matching mine.

At Dr. Andrews' office, I feel my nerves settle when I see both babies moving on the screen. They are alive and well, and so active. I glance at John and see the same look of awe on his face.

Dr. Andrews smiles at us. "Alright, are you ready to know the sexes?"

John squeezes my hand. "Tell us," he says eagerly.

"Baby A is a girl," Dr. Andrews announces, moving the wand slightly. "And Baby B... also a girl."

I gasped, tears welling in my eyes. "Two girls?"

John chuckles softly, but his voice cracks a little. "Two more little girls," he says, wiping his eyes. He never cries, but today... it is one of those moments.

I laugh through my tears. "I never thought I'd be here again—having more kids. We were done, John!"

"I know," he says, his voice low, filled with emotion. "But look at them. It's surreal."

As we leave the hospital, walking through the big glass foyer, the unthinkable happens. John collapses right in front of me. There is no warning, no time to react. He hit the marble floor hard, and I screamed, panicked. "Help! Someone, help!"

A nurse rushes over, quickly assessing him. She waves another nurse over, and before I know it, they have John on a gurney, wheeling him toward the ER. My heart races as I follow them, barely able to keep up.

In the ER, Dr. Cook approaches me. I recognize him—he was the one who saw Jon Wright after the accident. He is also the one who thought I was confused or out of my mind when I claimed Jon as my husband, John Hadley.

"Christi," Dr. Cook says, eyeing me with surprise. "You again?"

I nod, too overwhelmed to explain. I do not know how much time passes before I finally call Michael. When he arrives, he does not waste a second. He wraps me in a hug, holding me tightly.

He pulls back and looks me in the eyes, his face serious. "Christi, I need to tell you something, and it's not easy to hear."

My heart drops. "What is it?"

"John is... living on borrowed time," he says slowly, watching my reaction.

"What do you mean?" I gasp, shaking my head. "What's happening?"

"He's suffered severe head trauma," Michael continues, his voice heavy. "Specifically, to his brain. There's hemorrhaging, and they cannot operate. There's nothing they can do to stop the bleeding."

I blink rapidly, trying to process his words. "So... there's nothing they can do?"

"No, Christi. They have given him medication to help, but it is only a matter of time," Michael says, his voice soft, full of sadness.

I feel myself sinking, my thoughts racing. "Why didn't he tell me?" I whisper. "I need to be ready for this... for what's coming."

I think back to my dreams. The darkness, the sense of doom—Michael saving me every time. Hesitant, I glanced at him. "Have you... have you had any dreams about me?" I ask quietly.

Michael looks at me strangely, not answering.

"Michael?" I press, but he shakes his head, changing the subject abruptly.

"I took Jake and Shelby to your new house," he says, clearing his throat.

I frown, confused by the sudden shift. "What?"

"Luke and Chelsea are watching all the kids," he adds, avoiding my gaze. "They've got their hands full, but they'll manage."

I know they can manage it, but Michael's deflection leaves me feeling unsettled. Something is off, but I cannot quite put my finger on it. Still, I nod, too drained to push further.

CHAPTER 25

I sit beside John's hospital bed, my body aching from the uncomfortable chair. I have been here for hours, and my muscles are stiff. I need to stretch, but just as I am about to get up, John stirs. His eyes open, and they lock onto mine.

I lean forward, the question escaping my lips before I can stop it. "How much time do you have?"

John looks at me, his face weary. "I don't know," he says quietly, his voice hoarse. "I'm praying I have enough time... just to see the birth of our twin girls."

His words hit me like a punch to the chest. A sense of urgency I hadn't fully acknowledged before begins to overwhelm me. We need to name them. We need to prepare. How much time do we really have?

My thoughts race, and I think of Pam. "What about your mom? How is Pam going to handle this? She is more emotional than I am. She... she won't be able to hear this."

John looks away, pain flickering in his eyes. "I don't know, Christi. I haven't told her yet."

The room feels smaller, like the walls are closing in. I cannot stop the next question from tumbling out of my mouth. "Does this mean you and Jon Wright were both supposed to die that night? And you... you were just granted some kind of life extension?"

John's expression tells me he does not know the answer any more than I do. He shakes his head slowly. "I don't know. I've been asking myself that same question."

Frustration wells up in me, mingling with sadness. "I can't do this without you!" My voice cracks, and I press my hand to my mouth. "Why didn't you tell me sooner?"

He closes his eyes for a moment, gathering his thoughts before speaking. "I didn't want to add more stress to your life. I wanted to protect you, keep you happy... even if that meant keeping this from you."

"Keeping me happy?" I repeat, my voice softening. "Do you think finding out like this is any easier? You should have told me, John."

"I know," he admits, his voice barely a whisper. "I just... I didn't want to burden you."

I shake my head; tears sting my eyes. "We could have gotten a second opinion. A third. There has to be someone out there, some doctor willing to help, to save you."

John gives me a sad smile. "I'm not giving up, Christi. But sometimes... sometimes it's not in our hands."

I cannot accept that. I will not. He must stay in the hospital overnight, but I know it is just a formality. It feels so pointless—monitoring him when it's only a matter of time. But I do not want to waste a single minute. Not now.

I stand up slowly, leaning over to press a soft kiss to his forehead. "I'll be back tomorrow," I whisper, though it feels inadequate, like an empty promise in the face of everything that is happening.

John watches me leave; his eyes heavy with the weight of everything unsaid.

Outside, Michael is waiting for me. He is leaning against John's big Ford truck, the one I have not driven and won't even try to tonight. I am too exhausted to argue when he offers to take me home.

"Thanks for waiting," I say, sliding into the passenger seat.

He glances at me, concern etched across his face. "You doing, okay?"

I give a tired nod. "As okay as I can be, I guess."

We drive in silence for a while, the weight of everything pressing down on me. But I cannot stop myself. I have to know. I turned to him. "Michael, about the dreams... you've been dreaming about me, haven't you?"

Michael shifts uncomfortably, keeping his eyes on the road. "Yeah," he admits after a long pause. "I have."

"What are they about?" I ask, watching him closely.

He hesitates. "In most of them... I am saving you. From something. I don't always know what, but I'm always there, pulling you out of danger."

I blink, absorbing this. "Always saving me?"

Michael lets out a nervous laugh. "Yeah... and, uh, one dream... it was of our wedding day."

I stared at him, my breath catching. "Our wedding day?" I repeat, incredulous.

His cheeks flush, and he glances at me, clearly embarrassed. "I know it's weird," he says, running a hand through his hair. "I don't know why I'm dreaming about it."

He keeps apologizing, his words tumbling over each other. "I'm sorry, Christi. I did not mean to—"

"Stop apologizing," I interrupted him, placing a hand on his arm. "You don't need to be sorry. This... whatever this is... it is bigger than us. We're not in control."

Michael does not say anything, but his jaw tightens as he grips the steering wheel. I stared out the window, lost in thought.

"We get messages," I continue softly. "Maybe these dreams... maybe they're messages. Telling us what path to take or warning us about something. But all we can do is do our best... with what's thrown at us."

He nods, but neither of us speaks again as we drive the rest of the way in silence.

CHAPTER 26

All eight kids are outside laughing and splashing in the pool. Chelsea and Luke are sitting on the steps with their feet in the water, keeping an eye on the younger ones. The scene is peaceful, full of giggles and the sound of water slapping against the sides of the pool.

Luke glances over at Michael, who is standing near the edge, clearly lost in thought. With a mischievous grin, Luke pulls his feet out of the water and walks over. Without a word, he shoves Michael into the pool—clothes, wallet, and all.

"Luke!" Michael shouts as he splashes into the water, but the kids erupt in laughter, swarming him in the pool before he can do anything else.

Michael quickly shakes off the surprise and starts tossing the kids in every direction, their shrieks echoing through the backyard. "Alright, who's next?!" He laughs, playfully splashing them back.

I watch from the patio, smiling at their fun. The kids shout, "Mom, come join us!" Vince and Campbell wave me over, their hands already cupping water to splash.

I headed inside, slipping into my old swimsuit. It is not a maternity suit, but it still fits—barely. At five and a half months pregnant with twins, my belly's still small enough that I can manage it. I grab two towels, one for me and one for Michael, before stepping out to the pool.

As soon as I walked down the steps into the water, Vince and Campbell splashed me, grinning ear to ear. "Hey! I am not even in yet!" I laugh, wading deeper in. The water is warm, but the cool March air sends a shiver down my spine. Still, it is nice to relax, at least for a little while. None of the kids know about John being in the hospital. Right now, they are carefree, happy, and I want to keep it that way.

After about half an hour, Chelsea and Luke round up the younger ones, herding them toward the house. "Alright, bath time!" Chelsea announces, clapping her hands.

"I'm not tired yet!" Campbell protests, but Luke scoops him up over his shoulder, laughing.

"You will be after a hot shower," Luke teases, carrying him inside.

The kids' voices fade as the door closes, and suddenly, it is just me and Michael in the pool. The air feels different, heavier, but I know I need to talk to him. I swim over to the stairs where he is sitting.

"Michael... I have been having dreams." I hesitate for a second before continuing. "They've been so vivid, so real. In them, you are always saving me. I do not know if they're just dreams or if they mean something more."

Michael listens quietly, his face serious as I speak. When I finish, he leans back, thinking. "I don't know what I'm supposed to save you from," he says softly. "But I would do anything to keep you safe."

His words hung in the air between us, and I cannot help but blush. I look down at the water, trying to compose myself. But before I can say anything,

Michael moves toward me, gently pulling me closer. His hands find my waist, and he wraps my legs around him, my pregnant belly resting between us.

I laugh nervously. "What are you doing?" I ask, a half-smile on my lips.

Michael grins, his voice low. "I'm saving you from drowning in this pool."

I giggle, but before I can respond, it happens. His lips meet mine. The kiss is soft at first, gentle, but it deepens. His lips are warm and full, perfectly fitting over mine. The world around us seems to fade, leaving just the two of us.

But as the kiss lingers, reality crashes back into my mind. I pull away slowly, my breath shaky. "We can't do this," I whisper, but my voice wavers. The passion between us is undeniable, but so is the guilt.

Michael's face falls, and I can see the conflict in his eyes. He knows it too. I look down at my hands, thinking of John, lying in a hospital bed, brain bleeds threatening his life while I am here, letting this happen.

"I'm sorry," Michael whispers, his voice filled with regret.

I nod, swallowing hard. "We both are."

We stay like that for a moment, the weight of what just happened pressing down on both of us. The shame, the guilt—it is all there, but so is the truth. We care about each other more than we are willing to admit.

But it does not change the reality. John is still in that hospital, and I cannot let this happen. Not now. Not like this.

CHAPTER 27

Michael looks at me with an intensity I wasn't expecting. His voice is soft but filled with something deep, something raw. "Christi, I'm in love with you," he says, the words coming out slowly, deliberately. "I felt it the first time I saw you again, standing in Jon's living room. I know you love John, and I'm not asking you to betray him." He pauses, searching my eyes for understanding. "But he's dying, and he asked me to take care of you and the kids. I will do that, Christi. I will. But please... don't hate me."

I feel my breath catch in my throat. There is no anger in his voice—just pain, confusion, and a desperate need to be understood. I shake my head, trying to find the right words. "I don't hate you," I manage to say, my voice barely above a whisper. "I could never hate you." The truth is, I know I have feelings for him too, even if I do not want to admit it out loud.

We get out of the pool, both of us silent as we towel off, the impact of what just happened lingering in the cool night air. When we open the back door, we move quietly, making sure not to wake the kids upstairs. The house is peaceful, but inside, my thoughts are anything but.

Michael and I sit down on the sofa in the den. There is a warmth here, a familiarity in the way we sit together. He lights the fireplace, the soft crackling of the wood filling the room. For hours, we just talked about everything. The confusion swirled around us. The dreams we cannot make sense of.

Eventually, the exhaustion from the night takes over. I do not remember when I fell asleep, but I woke up around 4 a.m., the soft glow of the fire was almost gone. Michael is still beside me, sleeping on the sofa, his arm draped over the back. I pull a blanket over him and quietly slip away to my own bed, my heart heavy.

I lie down, staring at the ceiling, my mind racing. This situation is impossible. A dying husband who is not really my husband but looks like the man who killed him. And Michael—Jon's brother—who I am slowly falling for. It feels like a nightmare I cannot wake up from. How did I get here?

There is a party in ten hours, and I need to pull myself together. But instead, I fall back into a restless sleep, dreaming of John's funeral. No—Jon Wright's funeral. The one he never had. My mind keeps twisting reality, making everything feel surreal. When I wake up again, the shame is there, gnawing at me. I kissed Michael. It was not just a casual kiss, either— it was full of something deeper, something I'm not ready to confront. But then I remind myself... my husband technically died on December 3, 2012. And the man I call my husband now is dying all over again.

I try to justify it to myself. Dr. Andrews does not know. My friends do not know. My coworkers, my family—they all think John is just my boyfriend. No one knows the truth. No one knows the weight of the secret I am carrying.

There is a knock at the door. I freeze, wondering who it could be so early. When I open it, I am surprised to see John standing there. He is unexpected, but I don't hesitate. "Come in," I whisper, holding a finger to my lips. "The kids are still asleep."

He steps inside, his movements quiet but hurried. His eyes scan the room, landing on Michael, who is still asleep on the sofa. There is a flicker of something in John's expression—something hard, something like understanding, but also hurt. He does not say a word about it, but I can read him like a book. Even though this is not his real face, I know him too well to miss the silent message. He is not happy about Michael being here.

I lead John into the bedroom, and as soon as we are inside, he lies down on the bed without a word. I sit beside him, looking down at him. "What are you doing here? I thought you were still in the hospital."

John sighs, his voice low. "I wasn't discharged. I just... walked out. I could not stay there anymore, Christi. I am not wasting another minute of my life stuck in that place. I need to be here—with you, with the kids. I want to stay close to the babies."

His words hit me hard, and for a moment, all I could do was smile weakly. But the guilt from earlier starts creeping in, gnawing at the edges of my mind. I kissed Michael. How can I keep that from him? But I cannot tell him. Not now. Not when he is already dealing with so much. I swallow the lump in my throat.

"Well," I say, stifling a yawn, "let's sleep for an hour, and then we can get ready for the party." I try to sound casual, but my voice is shaky. John nods, his hand gently brushing my hair away from my face.

"Yeah, that sounds good," he murmurs.

I lay my head on his chest, the steady beat of his heart calming me. But my thoughts are anything but calm. This is too much. Too complicated. How am I supposed to deal with all of this?

Within minutes, I am asleep again, my head spinning with questions that I have no answers for.

CHAPTER 28

The alarm blares, piercing through the quiet, and I groggily reach for my phone, fumbling to find the snooze button. The house feels like a whirlwind as I get up, moving frantically from room to room. The party is today, and I am always extra anxious when guests are coming over.

I am in the middle of helping the younger kids get ready when Luke walks up to me, a strange expression on his face.

"What's wrong, Luke?" I ask, noticing the furrowed look in his brow.

He hesitates before blurting out, "Why did I just see Jon Wright in your bedroom?"

My stomach twists. There is no lie that would make this easier, no simple explanation. I glance at him, then sigh deeply. "Luke, I need to tell you the truth."

His face hardens as he crosses his arms. "What truth?"

I motion for Chelsea and Michael, calling them into Jan and Emily's room. "I need your help," I whisper to them. John walks in behind them, and we gather around Luke.

Taking a deep breath, I start, "Jon Wright... he's John Hadley. They are the same person."

Luke's eyes widen. "Are all of you messing with me, or are you all mental?"

Michael shifts uncomfortably but responds with a chuckle. "I know it sounds insane, but… Jon Wright's body is my brother's. But John, your John, is still here, in that body."

I nod, trying to make this as clear as possible. "It is not just us. The boys, John's mom, Pam—they all see it, Luke."

Luke's face is a mix of disbelief and shock. His voice is flat when he says, "I need you all to leave the room."

We all hesitate, but we slowly file out, unsure of what is going to happen. As soon as I step out, I stay close to the door, straining to hear anything.

A minute or two later, Luke emerges, his eyes red, wet with tears. He looks directly at me and says quietly, "I believe you."

I walk back into the room where John is waiting. "What did Luke say to you?"

John sits down, rubbing his face as if to process everything. "We had a man-to-man conversation just before the accident," he says softly. "Luke asked me to recall it, to prove who I was. When I did, he knew."

My curiosity itches at me, but I remember Luke had asked John to keep their talk private. "I promised not to tell anyone about it," John adds. "Not even you."

I nod slowly. "Fair enough. I will not ask."

Just then, Michael steps into the room. There is a tension between us, and I find it hard to meet his eyes. He turns to John. "We need to talk. Man to man."

I froze for a moment, worried about what Michael might say, but I gave them space. After all, they have got their own complicated bond now.

Sometime later, they both walk out, laughing and joking, seemingly putting everything behind them. Relief floods through me—Michael had not mentioned the kiss. At least, not now.

The party later is a tremendous success, though it leaves me utterly drained. The balloon arches around the pool were a hit, making everything feel festive, but I pushed myself too hard. By the end, I am running on fumes.

John asks me to stay the night at his place like I usually do on weekends, but tonight, I just need to be in my own bed.

"I really want you to stay with me," John says softly, his eyes filled with concern.

"I wish you could stay here, or I wish I could stay with you too," I admit. "But Jan and Emily do not know yet. I do not want to shock them or have to explain anything if they see I'm gone or that you are here in the morning."

John looks disappointed, but he understands. "Okay," he agrees. "I'll leave before they wake up."

We both know it is best not to traumatize anyone else in the family, not with everything that's already happened. Still, it is hard not to feel the hurt of keeping this secret, especially when so much has already spiraled out of control.

CHAPTER 29

John was replaying the events of the day in his mind. It felt strange to be at the party, surrounded by his dad and brothers, yet they had no idea who he really was. Pam hugged John discreetly when no one was looking at them.

"Your dad and brothers will know everything soon," she whispered, glancing around to make sure no one else could hear. "Just give them some time."

I wanted to say, *I hope it is sooner than later,* because John was living on borrowed time. As Michael and his kids prepared to leave for John's house in Taylor, he pulled me into a tight hug.

"Sweet dreams," he said, planting a soft kiss on my cheek.

"What does that even mean?" I wondered, confusion swirling in my mind. *Is this some kind of game to him?* Did he not realize how difficult this all was for me? I thought about how when John passes, I would be left with a total of eight children, and Michael has two of his own. *Are we supposed to raise ten kids together?* I shook my head, trying to push those thoughts aside.

Just as I settled into my king-sized comfortable bed, ready to fall asleep, John's voice broke the silence.

"You know Michael has fallen for you, don't ya?"

I feigned surprise, denying any knowledge of it.

"Really? He has?" I replied, trying to sound casual.

"Oh, yes. He confessed his undying love for you about a month ago when you were assisting him with his divorce settlement."

"Doesn't that make you angry with him?" I asked, feeling a knot tighten in my stomach.

John chuckled softly. "No. I know Michael is a good man. I find comfort in knowing he will take care of you and the kids after I… you know."

I blinked, taken aback. "You actually want him to take care of me? While you are...?"

John nodded, a bittersweet smile on his face. "I was hoping he'd wait until I was six feet under before he started spending quality time with you, though."

"This is all too weird for me," I admitted, feeling the weight of our conversation. "I cannot just be with Michael. What would people think? They would say I did not genuinely love you."

John shifted closer, his expression serious. "Christi, I do not care what others think. I know how much you love me. That is what matters."

"I know, I know," I sighed. "But it feels wrong. I do not want people to see me with the man responsible for your death, and then think I just moved on to his brother."

Silence enveloped us for a moment, the heaviness of our words lingering in the air. Then, John leaned in, kissing me with fierce passion.

"I miss your touch," I murmured against his lips, kissing him back with all the emotion I could muster. *Every kiss could be our last,* and we both knew it.

Tears welled up in my eyes as I held him close. "I don't want to take these moments for granted," I whispered. "Every second is special now."

John brushed my cheek with his thumb. "I love you," he said softly, and I felt his warmth seep into my very being.

As we kissed, I could not help but cry. John had always sported a Fu Manchu, but Jon Wright's face was clean-shaven. I traced where his mustache would have been and asked, "Can you grow it out? Just for me?"

"Of course," he replied, a playful smile on his lips. I snuggled closer, feeling content for a moment.

Suddenly, he jumped a little as he felt a kick from my belly. "Whoa! I do not know which one of you girls did that, but I suspect you are going to be a soccer player," he joked, moving down to kiss my baby bump.

"Goodnight, little ones," he said tenderly, speaking to the babies as if they could hear him.

He settled down with his head on my stomach, his hands resting gently on me. I did not want to move him; it felt so sweet. But I checked on him multiple times, my heart racing with the thought that he could slip away at any moment. I felt like a mother checking on her newborn, making sure he was still breathing.

CHAPTER 30

May 16, 2013, I'm at work sitting in a conference room with a potential new client, when suddenly, I feel a rush of warmth. My water breaks.

"Excuse me," I say, cutting off mid-sentence. "I need to step out for a moment."

I move quickly to the restroom, my heart racing. I pulled out my phone and called John, but there's no answer. I know he's at work, so I try Michael's cell instead.

"Michael!" I exclaim when he picks up. "You're having the babies, aren't you?"

"Yes, but how did you know? I'm still a few weeks from my due date!"

"I had another dream last night," he explains. "In it, you went into labor, and I was the one taking you to the hospital."

I can't help but laugh a little. "Well, you're right about one thing. I need to get to the hospital now."

"I'm on my way," he assures me. "I'll call John on my way there."

I tell one of the paralegals in my office to finish my consultation while I grab my things. Michael arrives in record time, and I'm grateful, though I'm worried about how fast he's driving.

"Just please don't speed!" I plead. "I'd rather not be in labor while you're getting pulled over."

When we arrived at the hospital, the nurse checked me, and I felt a strong urge to push. "I can't believe this is happening," I say, panic creeping in. "The girls weren't supposed to arrive for weeks!"

"You've got this," Michael encourages. "Just focus."

After only a few pushes, I hear a baby crying, and relief washes over me. "I did it!" I gasped, tears of joy streaming down my face. I look at John, who bursts into the room just as Baby A is placed in my arms.

"Is that our little girl?" John asks, his voice shaky with emotion as he leans closer.

"Yeah, it is. Isn't she beautiful?" I reply, kissing the baby's forehead.

I hear a nurse say, "Baby B is not positioned properly."

Just then, Dr. Andrews enters, and confusion fills the air. "Whoever is going into the surgical room with her needs to suit up quickly," he says, glancing between John and Michael.

"That's me," John says decisively, sliding off his shoes and putting on scrub pants over his slacks. He fumbles with the shoe covers as they wheel me away.

I look over at Michael, who gives me an encouraging nod.

Inside the surgical room, John sits beside my head, his hand gripping mine tightly. "Here we go!" he says, a mixture of excitement and nerves in his eyes.

As I feel pressure and hear the cries of another baby, I can't hold back my tears. "Is that…?"

"Yes, that's our second girl!" John grins, tears streaming down his cheeks.

"Do you want to cut the cord?" Dr. Andrews asks, and John nods eagerly.

"Absolutely!" John stands up and moves around the curtain. "I can't believe this is happening!"

Moments later, I'm back in the room where I delivered the first baby, and Michael is still holding her. "Congratulations!" he beams, handing her over to John.

"She's perfect," John whispers, looking down at our daughter. "What should we name her?"

"I always liked the name Ashley," I suggest, and Michael adds, "And what about Bella for Baby B?"

John and I exchanged glances. "Bella sounds perfect!" We both agree.

As I begin nursing Ashley, I feel overwhelmed with love. "I never imagined this moment would be so special," I say, glancing up at John, who is attempting to burp Bella.

"Me neither," he replies, his eyes shining with joy. "We're really doing this, aren't we?"

I'm in my mid thirties and I just gave birth to twins. I am very sore. The hospital will need to keep me for a few days, because of the second baby being born via cesarian.

Three days later, we're finally discharged from the hospital. John and I placed the twins in the truck, and we drove to our house.

When we arrived, Pam and Frank were at the house to greet us.

"Why is Jon Wright here with you?" Frank asks, raising an eyebrow as he notices the empty guest chair.

"Dad," John starts, but Frank cuts him off.

"Don't you dare call me that! You are not half the man my son was," he retorts, anger flaring in his voice. "I won't let you encroach on my son's family."

"Dad, please," John pleads, his expression softening. "There's something you need to understand…"

CHAPTER 31

Pam and I exchanged worried glances, silently agreeing it was time to tell Frank the truth.

John, however, broke the tension, "August 15, 2001, we went to the Joy Nightclub for my 21st birthday, remember? You told Mom we were on a hunting trip. We joked that we were hunting all right, but not for deer—"

"Stop right there," Frank interrupted, glaring at John. "What are you saying? You were at a strip club?"

John nodded. "Yeah. I was at the strip club with you. You surprised me with my first lap dance. You made me promise never to tell Mom the truth, but given the circumstances—"

"Given that you're supposed to be dead," I added, trying to lighten the mood a bit.

"Exactly!" John continued. "So that promise is invalid now. I was not ready to die on December 3, 2012. I was not ready to say goodbye to my family. I did not get a chance to say goodbye."

"What are you talking about?" Frank's brows furrowed, clearly confused.

"I bartered with the other guy in the accident," John said, his tone serious. "People can see me. My wife can see me. Mom can see me. Chelsea can too. Recently, even the boys and Luke can see me. So why can't you, Dad? Why can't you see the real me?"

Frank's face twisted in frustration. "This is not a joke, Jon! You think this is funny?"

"No, it's not funny! I'm right here," John insisted, gesturing towards himself. "I'm still your son."

Frank crossed his arms, looking more upset by the second. "What is this nonsense? You're not my son. You're just—"

"Wait," John interjected, his voice steady. "Let me share another secret. When I was sixteen, I broke the side mirror off Mom's car while backing out of the garage."

Frank's expression shifted, a mix of confusion and surprise. "Anyone could have known about that."

"Yeah, but you told Mom and the insurance company that a random idiot must have hit it while the car was parked at the grocery store. Remember?" John continued, the memories flowing back to him.

Frank's eyes widened. "I thought my son was going to keep that a secret forever!"

John chuckled softly. "Well, I guess I'm not keeping secrets anymore, Dad. You told me once that Christi was the greatest thing that could have happened to me. You told me not to listen to your original advice."

I could see the hurt flash across John's face as he shared these memories, and I felt a twinge of anger at Frank for the pain he'd caused.

Suddenly, Frank stood up, his face flushed. "I can't do this right now." He walked out of the room, leaving the air heavy with unspoken tension.

"Well, that was awkward," I said, breaking the silence that hung in the room.

Pam sighed deeply, glancing at the door where Frank had exited. "He's just shocked. This is a lot to take in."

"I'm more worried about the stripper thing," I said, glancing at the cribs where the twins were beginning to wail. "And I've got two hungry, crying babies now."

Pam nodded; concern etched across her face. "Let me help with the girls. John, come on, let's go."

John and Pam left the room, and I was left alone with the twins. I cradled one in each arm, feeling the load of the moment press down on me. How was I going to explain this new guy staying in our home to Jan and Emily? How could I let them bond with John again, knowing they would experience another loss?

It felt so unfair to all of us.

CHAPTER 32

Frank and Pam entered our bedroom. John gently cradles Ashley, who continues to cry, her tiny face scrunching up in discomfort. Pam, with her warm smile, walks over and softly says, "Let me take her for a moment, John."

John hesitates, looking at the little girl as if she holds the entire world in her hands. "Are you sure, Mom? I want to be the one to soothe her."

"I've got this, sweetheart," Pam reassures him, taking Ashley gently. "You need to rest too. You've been through so much."

John finally relinquishes Ashley, and she calms instantly in Pam's embrace. Frank stands to the side, arms crossed, his expression a mix of concern and disbelief. "I just can't wrap my head around all this," he mutters, shaking his head slightly.

"I know it's a lot to take in, Dad," John says, trying to keep his tone light, "but I'm still here, and I want to be part of this family. I want to be with you all."

Frank nods but keeps his gaze on the floor, wrestling with his emotions. "It's just... you were gone, John. We buried you. Now, seeing you like this—" His voice catches, and he sighs deeply. "It's confusing."

"I understand, but you have to believe me. I'm still your son," John insists, a hint of desperation in his voice.

"Your body looks different," Frank replies, a frown deepening on his forehead. "I see Jon Wright's face, not yours."

"I get that. But look past the surface, Dad," John pleads.

Frank runs a hand through his hair, clearly torn. "You weren't ready to die. You bartered with the other guy in the accident?"

"Yeah," John nods. "I wanted to stay, to say goodbye to everyone, especially you.

Frank looks stricken, his emotions swirling. "This isn't how it should be. You shouldn't be here like this."

"I agree. But I'm here. Again, I want to be with my family, and that includes you," John insists.

"Accept me for who I am now," John says earnestly. "I'm still your son, even if my body looks different."

Frank smiles with a face of acceptance. He hugs John and decides to believe all of us.

As I prepare to feed the twins again, Frank, Pam and John excuse themselves, leaving me to face the next challenge. I can't help but feel a pinch of worry. The love and laughter surrounding us right now are so precious, but I know the storm is brewing just beneath the surface.

CHAPTER 33

Frank recognized Michael from the pool party. "Hey, you're that guy from the pool party, right?" Frank said, raising an eyebrow as he eyed Michael.

"Yeah, that's me," Michael replied with a half-smile. "And you're Frank, if I'm not mistaken."

"Correct. So, what's your deal with John? I find it curious you're living with him in Taylor." Frank leaned back against the kitchen counter; arms crossed.

Michael shrugged, glancing around the room. "It's complicated. We're trying to help each other out, I guess."

Frank raised an eyebrow, skepticism evident on his face. "Complicated? It seems to me John and Christi should be working together in the same house with the kids. Why the separation?"

"Trust me, it's ironic," I interjected, a hint of frustration creeping into my voice. "I want my husband with me, but I don't want him with me."

Frank cut in, shaking his head. "Why not bring him in?"

I sighed, feeling the weight of the situation. "I honestly don't know how this is going to work with John staying here. We're just figuring it out as we go."

Frank nodded, his expression softening. "Well, I'll be in San Antonio tomorrow. I just need to get a little rest before my next shift."

"Got it. It's been a long day," I said, trying to sound reassuring. "Tonight is our first night at home with the girls. I have a couple of bottles of breast milk ready, so John can help out during the night. Pam's always willing to lend a hand too."

Frank smirked. "At least you have a plan. The kids go back to school tomorrow, right? You think you will have enough energy to manage all that?"

I chuckled nervously. "I am praying for it. But Pam is reading my mind. She just told me she will get all the kids ready and drive them to school. All I must worry about are the twins."

"That sounds like a lovely plan," Frank said, sounding relieved.

As we chatted, Michael was getting ready to leave with Jake and Shelby. Just as they reached the door, I noticed my ex-husband, Royce, staggering on the front porch.

"Royce!" I called out, dread pooling in my stomach as he squinted in the sunlight.

"What is this? You got a party going on without me?" he slurred, swaying slightly.

"Michael's just leaving, Royce," I said, trying to keep my tone steady. "Let him go."

Royce's eyes narrowed as he stepped closer, focus zeroing in on Michael. "What the hell are you doing here? You think you can just come into my home?"

John stepped outside, instinctively moving to my side. He placed his hand on the small of my back, a protective gesture that made me feel safer. "I think it's time for you to leave," John said firmly, his voice steady.

Michael chimed in, "Yeah, I second that motion."

Royce let out an evil chuckle, sending a chill down my spine. "You think you can just throw me out like that? I'm still their father!"

I knew that laugh all too well; it sent shivers down my neck. "Royce, just go home. You're not making this any better," I urged.

Suddenly, with a wild swing, Royce raised a stick and WHAM! He struck John on the head.

"John!" I screamed, my heart racing as he crumpled to the ground.

Michael lunged at Royce, fists flying. "Get away from him!" he yelled, landing a punch squarely on Royce's face.

"Help! Somebody help!" I shouted, panic flooding my voice.

Pam rushed outside; her eyes wide as she took in the scene. "What happened?" she gasped, dropping to John's side.

"I don't know! I checked his pulse—he's alive!" I cried, desperation creeping in. "But he's not moving!"

Pam fumbled with her phone, her hands shaking. "I need to call 911!"

"John, can you hear me? Please, wake up!" I pleaded, tears streaming down my face.

Just then, Pam saw her chance. She kicked Royce in the head, and he finally went limp. "Stop! Just stop moving!" she shouted, her voice filled with adrenaline.

"John, please!" I begged, shaking his shoulder gently. "You have to be okay!"

The police arrived before the EMTs, and I could see the officers swiftly handcuffing Royce. "Good riddance," I muttered, feeling a mix of relief and anger.

When the ambulance finally arrived, the EMTs moved too slowly for my comfort. They began working on John, and Pam said, "I'm riding with him."

"I can't argue with that," I replied, swallowing hard. "I've got the twins to think about." I leaned down, pressing a kiss to John's cheek. "I love you," I whispered, tears pouring down my face.

As the chaos began to settle, my adrenaline faded, leaving me drained. Michael and his kids were staying the night, and I felt an unexpected sense of gratitude. "Thank you for helping with the kids," I said to Michael, voice trembling.

"No problem. I'll take them to school," he replied, determination in his eyes.

I called Pam for an update. The ER was still evaluating John. I asked her to call me if anything changed. Then, I stepped into the shower, the hot water washing away the remnants of the day. I wept, feeling the weight of my worries for John and myself. "I just want a normal life," I thought, feeling overwhelmed.

Once I stepped out, I found Michael watching the twins, who were blissfully asleep. "You need rest," he said softly. "Let me help."

I nodded, feeling a mix of gratitude and disbelief. "I don't know how you'll manage it all but thank you."

As I sank into bed, exhaustion washed over me. "I just need to sleep while I can," I thought about John and I anxiously waited for an update. It was difficult for me to stay home and not be by his side. I was thinking about John as I was drifting off into a deep slumber, grateful for the unexpected support around me.

CHAPTER 34

I woke briefly, hearing the sounds of corralling eight children for school. Chelsea and Luke, the older ones, could manage most things on their own, but I heard Michael giving them the occasional nudge.

"Chelsea, time to get up!" Michael called from down the hall. "Luke, don't fall back asleep after you brush your teeth."

From the faint murmur of voices, I could tell Emily, our little momma hen, was already on top of things. Her voice was soft but assertive.

"Vince, you must brush your teeth. Campbell, hurry up! We do not have all day," Emily instructed.

I smiled at the thought of Emily being a mother one day. Her nurturing side was shining through, even now.

As I lay there, the sounds of bustling kids leaving for school faded, and I started getting myself ready. My heart was heavy; I needed to see John as soon as possible. The thought of him lying in the hospital gnawed at me. I called Pam for an update, my fingers trembling as I dialed her number.

"Pam, how is he doing? Any news?" I asked, trying to mask the anxiety in my voice.

There was a brief pause before she responded, her tone somber. "It's not looking good. The doctors are doing everything they can, but... well, it's complicated. The blow to his head was bad."

I swallowed hard, trying to keep the panic from rising in my chest. "I'll be there as soon as I can. Can you stay with the babies for a while?"

"I'll be there in ten minutes," Pam said.

When I arrived at the hospital, Pam was waiting in the lobby. She gave me a quick hug and took the twins from me. "Go," she urged. "I'll keep an eye on them. You need to be with John."

I walked into John's room, my heart pounding in my chest. He looked so still, so different from the vibrant man I had fallen in love with. I sat beside him, wanting him to wake up. And when he did, his eyes blinked open slowly, but something was off.

"John?" I said softly, leaning forward.

He frowned, blinking up at me. "Who... who are you?"

My stomach dropped. "What do you mean? I'm— I'm your wife."

He looked confused, his brow furrowing deeper. "Wife? My name is John... Hadley?" he said, the uncertainty in his voice surprising me.

One of the ICU nurses glanced at me, then turned to him with a more neutral expression. "Your name is Jon Wright," she corrected.

John looked back at me, his confusion only growing. "You don't know my last name?"

I tried to explain, but the words caught my throat. My eyes filled with tears as I stammered, "I— it's just that..." I couldn't bring myself to tell the truth.

And then, suddenly, I heard a faint cry, distant but pulling me out of the nightmare. I blinked, realizing that it wasn't John's confused face in front of me, but the soft cries of Ashley coming from the nursery.

I shook my head, disoriented. It was just a bad dream. I got up quickly and went to check on Ashley. Her little face was scrunched up, tears streaming down her cheeks. I scooped her into my arms and rocked her gently, comforting her. I changed her diaper and placed her beside me on the bed, letting her nurse as I lay there, still shaken from the dream.

Then Bella started crying, her wail piercing through the quiet room.

A knock on the door followed. "Come in," I called, keeping my voice low.

Michael stepped in quietly, heading straight for Bella. "I've got her," he said, giving me a reassuring smile. He changed her diaper before carrying her over to the bed. "Here," he said, placing her beside me. "I'll burp Ashley."

As grateful as I was for his assistance, there was an undeniable awkwardness hanging in the air. I sat there, exposed, nursing the twins, and while Michael didn't seem to mind, I felt a flush creep up my neck.

He laid Ashley back in her cradle after burping her, then turned to me. "I'm going to call Pam and check on John," he whispered.

I nodded, my throat tight. "Okay, thank you."

After finishing with Bella, I placed her in her cradle and joined Michael in the den. He was sitting on the couch, his phone pressed to his ear. Pam's voice echoed faintly through the speaker.

"He's still in surgery," she said. "The blow caused massive internal bleeding in his brain. They're trying to stop it, but... the damage is severe. He already had some areas they couldn't fix because the surgery would've been too risky. This just made it worse."

I sank into the couch beside Michael, the severity of her words crashing down on me. "They can't fix it?"

Pam was quiet for a moment. "I don't know if he'll ever be the same, even if he makes it through this."

I couldn't think straight, the fear of losing John overshadowing everything else. "I can't sleep," I muttered, more to myself than to anyone.

Michael glanced at me, his face softening. "I don't blame you."

We sat in silence for a while, the weight of it all settling in. After a moment, Michael spoke, breaking the tension. "You know, it's kind of funny. You've got two kids with one crazy guy, two kids with another, and now two kids with... well, a guy in a body that doesn't even belong to him."

Despite everything, I found myself laughing. It was absurd, really. "It's like something out of a bad soap opera," I said, shaking my head. "But here we are."

Michael chuckled. "I mean, your life could be the next big telenovela."

For the first time in days, I allowed myself to smile. "Yeah, well, at least it keeps things interesting."

We laughed for a few moments longer before the heaviness returned. As sweet as Michael was, my heart belonged to John. Always had. Always would. No matter how complicated or surreal this life had become, I couldn't forget the life we had before everything changed.

"I loved him," I whispered, more to myself than to Michael. "We had something... almost perfect."

Michael didn't say anything, just nodded, respecting my space to grieve. I thought back to the anniversary trips, the spontaneous getaways, the way John always found a way to make me feel loved. We celebrated every moment, even the anniversary of our first date. John wasn't a hopeless romantic, but he knew I was, and he loved me in his own way, the way that counted.

Tears welled in my eyes as I thought about how much I missed him. "I don't want to live this life without him," I whispered, my voice cracking. "I don't know how to."

Michael reached over and gently touched my arm. "You won't have to," he said softly. "One way or another, we'll figure this out."

I nodded, appreciating his words, even if I could not fully believe them.

CHAPTER 35

The next morning, Michael handled the morning chaos like he's done it for years. I hear the usual rustling as he rounds up his kids and my four fledglings for school.

Chelsea grabs her bag and heads to campus. Luke, ever the independent one, waves goodbye as he drives himself off. Meanwhile, I am in the nursery, dressing the twins and trying to muster the energy to face another day at the hospital. I can't remember the last time I felt rested.

Michael calls from the hallway, "You ready? Car's packed and waiting."

I glance at Ashley and Bella, already in their little carriers, and nod. "Let's go." My voice sounds weaker than I'd like, but I can't fake it anymore. I'm exhausted.

The drive is quiet. Michael's hands grip the steering wheel as I sit in the back with the girls. His eyes flicker in the rearview mirror, concern etched in his face. He's taken FMLA leave for John's stay in the hospital, and I can tell it weighs heavily on him too.

When we arrive, the hospital air feels heavier than usual. John looks awful—swollen, pale. His body, his face… it's all Jon Wright. I swallow hard, the bad dream from last night swirling back into my thoughts. I catch Pam's eyes as she walks into the room. Her face mirrors my fear, though she doesn't say it. She doesn't have to.

The attending physician enters with a clipboard, his expression grim. "I won't sugarcoat this," he says, flipping through his notes. "His H-count is dangerously low. We'll need another transfusion. The internal damage... it's extensive."

I grip the edge of John's bed, feeling like I'm about to crumble. "Will he...?" My voice falters.

The doctor shakes his head. "I'm surprised he survived the surgery. He's in a very critical state."

Pam lets out a choked sob beside me. I can feel her panic radiating off her, but I don't have the energy to comfort her. All I can think is that John might never wake up again.

The next few days blur together. Between hospital visits, watching the babies, and trading shifts with Michael and Pam, I am running on fumes. Today, Frank is in town. He is taking his turn at John's bedside while I try to catch my breath at home.

Then, the call comes.

"He opened his eyes!" I practically scream into the phone. "John's awake!"

Pam and Michael are at the hospital in record time. When they rush into the room, John is barely conscious but alert enough to see them. The nurse removes his breathing tube, and he coughs, struggling to get words out.

"Water," he rasps, his hand weakly motioning toward the glass.

I help him sip slowly, trying to keep my hands steady. "John... how do you feel?"

He locks eyes with me, his voice barely a whisper. "Christi, I love you so much." Each word feels like a gift. "I'm thankful for these last six months... with you and the kids. I love you more than anything. Our girls… they're perfect, just like you."

Tears spill down my cheeks, and I squeeze his hand. "I love you too, John. So much."

He turns to Michael, "his brother."

"You're a good man, a good brother," he says, his voice weaker but determined. "Take care of them— our family."

Michael's jaw tightens. He cannot speak, so he just nods, his eyes wet. I have never seen him look so vulnerable.

Frank comes back in as Michael steps out, and John manages to smile for him and Pam. "I love you both," he says. "Thank you… for everything. Please, help Christi with the kids. Help her..."

Pam is sobbing, and even Frank is fighting back tears. I held John's hand tighter, not ready to say goodbye, not again.

John looks back at me, his eyes soft. "Tell all the kids I love them," he says. "Tell them every day. I'll be waiting for you… in Heaven. Watch the video I made for you."

I lean in, my forehead touching his. "I will. I'll never forget. I love you, John. Always."

He closes his eyes, and the room feels unbearably still.

I open the door, calling out to Michael. "Bring the girls in here."

Michael hesitates, knowing it's against the rules, but one look at my face and he doesn't argue. He returns with Ashley and Bella, placing them gently on John's chest.

John's head lifts just slightly, enough to kiss each of them. "I love you, girls…" His voice is barely a whisper now.

Pam kisses him on the forehead, whispering her own goodbye. We all say it— "I love you"—over and over, as if that could somehow keep him with us longer.

Michael steps forward, his voice breaking. "I love you, bro. Tell Jon and Debbie we said hi."

John smiles one last time. It is a peaceful smile. The kind that says he is ready.

And then the monitor beeps, that awful flat-line sound echoing in the room.

I freeze, my heart dropping into the pit of my stomach. Michael and I each take one of the babies, holding them close. It is over. John is gone. Again.

I do not even know how I made it out of the hospital. I am numb, walking on autopilot. Michael takes the car seats for me, and I follow behind him like a ghost. I cannot think, can't feel anything but the crushing weight of loss. I have lost John for the second time, and this time, there's no coming back.

We piled into Michael's car, leaving our vehicles behind for now. No one speaks, the silence heavy with grief. Michael starts the engine, and as the hospital fades from view, I try to block out the last few hours. I cannot handle it yet.

I know I need to keep going, for the babies, for all the kids, but right now, I feel utterly hollow.

I also have a busy law firm that needs me to have my head in the game. I will not let my clients suffer, because I have lost my husband. I am thinking about a number of things I need to focus on. I must be strong for so many people. I am having all these strange thoughts running through my mind. I'm also thinking about… I hear a knock on my door.

CHAPTER 36

Pam knocked on my bedroom door, peeking her head in. Her face mirrored my own confusion and worry. For once, she did not have the energy to do anything.

The thoughts that must have been running through her head could fill a novel.

"Hey," Pam said softly, stepping inside. "I don't know what to do either."

I nodded, knowing exactly how she felt. "It's strange, isn't it? Just… being in the quiet."

Pam sat down on the edge of the bed, fiddling with her fingers, something she never did unless she was deeply troubled. "We talked about Vince and Campbell staying with you," she continued, her voice uncertain. "I think… I think that is what's best. For them, you know?"

I sighed, thinking about it. "Yes, I want to keep the boys here. It just makes sense. They are already used to being here with the girls."

Pam gave me a small, understanding smile, though I could tell she was holding back her emotions. "I know they'd be better off here, with the rest of the kids," she agreed. "And don't worry. I'm not fighting you on this. I know it's what they need right now."

Her reassurance felt like a weight lifted, but that didn't make telling Vince and Campbell about John any easier. My heart sank at the thought of telling them, for a second time, that their daddy wouldn't be coming back.

The kids were due to ride the bus home that afternoon, and I dreaded the conversation that was waiting for me.

I reached for my phone and called Michael, needing his support. As soon as he answered, I didn't even let him say hello before blurting out, "Can you help me with the funeral arrangements?"

There was a brief pause before Michael responded. "Of course. Whatever you need, I'm here."

"I just... I don't know if I can do it again," I said, tears welling up in my eyes. "I already did this six months ago. For the same person, but in a different body. How am I supposed to get through this twice?"

Michael's voice was calm, as always. "We'll get through it together, okay? This time, we'll honor both John and Jon. We'll make it right."

I sighed, comforted by his words, but I knew this would be harder than anything I had faced before.

Suddenly, I heard Pam's muffled sobs from the next room. My heart clenched, and I quickly got up, ready to comfort her. As I made my way to her...

I woke up.

The sound of Bella crying pierced through the remnants of my dream. I jolted upright in bed, disoriented, my heart racing. Pam wasn't crying—none of that had happened. It was just another nightmare.

John wasn't dead! I repeated it to myself like a mantra, trying to steady my breathing. He was still in the hospital, alive. I scrambled off the bed and ran into the living room, half-expecting to find Michael gone, but he was still there, asleep on the sofa.

It was all a dream.

I picked up my phone with shaky hands and called Pam. Her voice was a welcome relief on the other end of the line.

"Christi, John's out of surgery," Pam said quickly, her tone filled with cautious optimism. "The doctor was able to stop the bleeding. He's going to be okay!"

A huge wave of relief washed over me, and I nearly dropped the phone. "He's... he's, okay?" I asked, my voice trembling.

"Yes. He's going to live."

Tears sprang to my eyes as I turned to the sound of Bella still crying from the nursery. My heart was racing, but this time with joy. We could still have the life I'd dreamed of.

At 6:30 a.m., Michael poked his head into my room. "Rise and shine!" he called, his voice cheerful.

I gave him a weak smile, still running on adrenaline and relief, but I was too afraid to sleep. Every time I closed my eyes, I saw John's lifeless body.

"You, okay?" Michael asked, noticing my face.

"I'll be fine," I lied. "Let's just get the kids ready for school."

Together, we woke all the kids, helped them get dressed, and rushed to make breakfast. The babies stayed home with Chelsea for a few hours while we dropped the other kids off at school.

We made our way to the hospital, my heart pounding with a mix of anxiety and hope.

When we entered John's hospital room, the sight of him awake, smiling, brought me to tears. I rushed to his bedside.

"I love you, John Hadley," I whispered, leaning over the bedrail to kiss him, pouring all my relief and love into that one kiss. I told him about the nightmares I had and he told me that everything he said in my dreams, was exactly how he felt. We did not know how much time John had left on this earth, but we were grateful for the memories we created during this borrowed time. We joked about taking pictures with the girls and pasting his real face onto Jon Wright's body. That is not a joke. I should really do that. I made sure to bring the girls to see John as much as I could while he was staying in the hospital.

One week later, John was finally being discharged from the hospital. Pam was home with the twins, and I had John's beloved truck waiting outside, knowing how much he adored it. As we walked through the door of our house, everyone was there to welcome him home. The kids ran to him, giving out hugs like they hadn't seen him in months.

John grinned and scooped Ashley up from the blanket on the floor, kissing her tiny forehead. Then he leaned over to kiss Bella, who was nestled in Pam's arms.

The love and joy in the room were palpable.

That night, we celebrated with a big barbecue in the backyard, grilling steaks and splashing around in the pool. I wrapped my legs around John's waist in the water, careful not to hurt him as I kissed him softly.

"What did Jan say to you?" I asked, remembering the moment from earlier when she had whispered in his ear.

John smiled. "She said, 'We know who you are because Vince and Campbell told us.'"

I smiled back, feeling a deep sense of contentment. The world might see John as Jon Wright, but the people who mattered most saw him for who he truly was—John Hadley.

But even in that perfect moment, my mind drifted back to the kiss with Michael, and guilt gnawed at me. I had to tell John about it.

Later, after the party had ended and Michael had taken his kids back to Taylor, John and I curled up in bed together. The twins were fast asleep, and we spooned comfortably under the covers.

"John," I said softly, breaking the peaceful silence. "There's something I need to tell you."

He shifted behind me, his arm wrapped securely around my waist. "I'm listening."

I swallowed hard, feeling my throat tighten. "One night, when Michael was over… we kissed. In the pool. I made a bad choice."

John was quiet for a moment, then he said, "I already knew about that."

I rolled over, staring at him in shock. "You… you knew?"

"Michael told me weeks ago," John said calmly.

"Why didn't you say anything?" I asked, feeling the guilt rise again.

"I knew you'd tell me when you were ready," he replied, his voice filled with understanding.

Tears welled up in my eyes. "I am so sorry, John. I thought I was going to lose you, and I was angry. And scared."

John smiled softly, brushing a strand of hair from my face. "I get it. It has been a lot to manage. But we are okay. We are together."

His words wrapped around my heart like a warm blanket, and for the first time in weeks, I felt a sense of peace. John has always been a calm person. I have always been the person to worry about the future. John has always lived one day at a time. Now, I see why we should all live one day at a time.

CHAPTER 37

In the morning, John and I wake up early, ready to tackle the day. We both get the kids ready for school. John, insisting on helping, heads to the kitchen to make his signature breakfast—eggs over medium, smothered with his special seasoning. It's a running joke that he always goes overboard with the spices, but the kids love it.

"I think you missed a spot," I tease, watching him sprinkle seasoning with a flourish.

"Just adding a little flair. The kids can't get enough of my eggs," he replies with a grin, nudging me playfully.

As much as he wants to drive the kids to school, I put my foot down. "There's no way I'm letting you drive after your surgery, John. Let's not add *another* visit to the hospital."

He sighs dramatically but gives in. Chelsea steps up and agrees to drive them, sparing us the argument.

Once the house is quiet, I decide to make a special breakfast just for John. After preparing his favorite meal, I carry it to him in bed. He sits up, eyes lighting up when he sees the tray.

"You spoil me," he says with a warm smile.

"I try," I reply, settling down beside him. As we eat, we start talking about the future. John mentions something that's been on our minds for a while.

"I think I'll move into this house," he suggests, "and Michael can have Jon's place. It's only right, considering he's the sole beneficiary. Plus, I think Michael could use the space."

I nod, understanding the logic. "It makes sense. We don't need Jon's house—between the money from the accident lawsuit and the life insurance policies, we're fine."

Then, with a mischievous grin, John asks, "So, are we going to live in sin, or do you want to marry Mr. Wright? Get it? Mr. *Right*?"

I laugh, but the question lingers in the air. What's the best decision for us, for the girls, for Vince and Campbell? What will Ashley and Bella know about John Hadley or Jon Wright as they grow older? I'm not sure, but I guess we'll have to figure it out together.

John makes a call to Michael to update him on our plans. I can't help but feel a twinge of guilt. I know Michael had feelings for me, and with everything going on, he probably thought that John wouldn't make it. That in time, *we* would be together. His dreams had led him to believe that.

After the call, we shift our thoughts to other matters, like the case against Royce. With four charges, including attempted murder, he's not getting out anytime soon. Jan and Emily don't know what their father did, and I'm not sure how to tell them. They're bound to have questions, especially as Royce's absence becomes more noticeable.

As the day slips into a peaceful lull, John and I take a nap while the twins are asleep. When we wake, our conversation turns to the idea of a wedding—or more accurately, a vow renewal. It's a technicality, a legal formality, but it feels important to us.

"I want it to be special," I say, imagining the day. "A big, white dress. Lots of friends and family. Eight to ten bridesmaids with me, standing up there with you."

John chuckles, nodding in agreement. "Yeah, I want it to be a celebration."

But before we could go any further, John suddenly collapses to the floor. My heart stops. I *know* what this means—he's gone. For a moment, I can't breathe, paralyzed by the realization. It's like my worst fear has come true, and no matter how many times I've braced myself for this moment, it still hits like a tidal wave.

I drop to my knees beside him, shouting his name, shaking him. "John! John!" But deep down, I know. I knew this was coming. We were living on borrowed time. Still, I can't stop myself from dialing 911 and performing CRP. It's pointless, but I must try. I know they can't save him. This is it.

Planning another funeral for the same man in a different body—it's unimaginable. This time it's for real. Michael steps in, aiding me in the planning of the service. It's small and intimate, just like before. And it rains, just like it did on the day of John's first funeral. Jon Wright's coworkers and old friends attend his service. I feel silly crying at the service for the man who killed my husband. I know I am truly morning John again, but others in attendance don't know that.

Weeks later, Michael and I decided to take all the kids on vacation. We need a break from the grief, from the weight of loss. We need to celebrate life instead of dwelling on what is gone. It is summer, and we have time. A month-long trip to Hawaii sounds like the perfect escape.

We arrived in Kihei, Maui, and rented a house for the month. Yesterday, Michael and I woke up early and had a cup of coffee on the patio of our rental house. The kids were all asleep, but we watched the sunrise together. The rest of the day, we spent the day at the beach with all the kids, soaking in the sun.Today,we had breakfast at Kihei Café. Their pancakes—drenched in coconut syrup—were divine. The omelets were perfect too.

Today, we are going on a submarine tour. As we walk to the dock in Lahaina, we pass the most incredible tree I have ever seen. It is an enormous banyan tree, almost 150 years old, shading the town square. We take a moment to rest on the benches beneath it, feeding pigeons as we soak in its beauty.

Eventually, we make our way to the dock and board the boat. The submarine crew greeted us, and we received a safety briefing. One of the crew members makes a joke about not needing a safety briefing, because if things go wrong underwater…. Most of the people on the submarine find him to be humorous. His comments make me feel anxious. But, before long, we are descending 130 feet below the surface. The ocean unfolds before us, teeming with fish and even some resting sharks. The captain tells us about a sunken boat that now serves as a habitat for coral and marine life. The kids are fascinated, and I'm thankful for this day, for this break. I'm thankful for the nanny watching Ashley and Bella, because it's difficult to do these things with this many kids and especially with babies.

After all that has happened, it feels good to watch the kids laugh and explore. We still have a trip to the island of Kauai. It will be an amazing week as well, but for now, we are enjoying Maui. For the time being, Michael and I are just friends. We both know it's too soon to even think about anything more. But someday, I know he will be my *Mr. Wright*.

John will always be in my heart, but I know he would want me to be happy. He lived and died trying to make sure of that.

About the Author

Melody Hadden is married to her husband, Josh. Melody and Josh have a total of six children and five grandchildren together. Melody and her husband own a busy roofing company. When they aren't assisting homeowners with their roofing needs, they are traveling or enjoying their spare time on their land with their children and grandchildren. Melody coaches junior high volleyball and she has also become a full-time writer.